Madeline watched the ma— Y0-DDS-862 toward her. The little boy's resemblance to her brother Scott sent chills through her entire body. Then Madeline really looked at the adult rider; suddenly she had a hard time catching her breath. In fact, she had a hard time doing anything but stare. Her eyes took in his dark hair pulled back in a ponytail, then rested for a moment on the mustache curving down over his upper lip. Madeline wondered how that mustache would feel if this man kissed her. Reluctantly she wrenched her eyes from his face; her gaze wandered over his broad shoulders and narrow hips. A flush suffused her features as she checked out the man's tight fitting jeans and a mental image of him standing in front of her minus everything but his hard male strength, flashed across her mind.

When she could trust herself to speak, Madeline started down the steps. She hoped the man didn't notice the glowing red spots on her cheeks.

"May I help you?" she asked, struggling to keep her voice under control. Her insides threatened to betray the outer calm she was fighting to project.

Devil In Her Arms

by

Patty Hardin

To Birdie,
What a ride! Thank
This has been!
you for your support!
Patty Hardin

Devil In Her Arms

Contact Information: info@thewildrosepress.com

Cover Art by *Kim Mendoza*

The Wild Rose Press
PO Box 706
Adams Basin, NY 14410-0706
Visit us at www.thewildrosepress.com

Publishing History
First Champagne Rose Edition, 2007
Print ISBN 1-60154-103-1

Published in the United States of America

Dedication

To the members, past and present, of the Willapa Writers
Circle, the members of Coastal Writers Critique, and my
husband who is the hero in my corner

Prologue

Madeline Spencer lowered herself to the soft grass, tucking her legs under her skirt. The early morning air was already heavy with the scent of flowers. She trailed her fingertips over the headstone, just like she had done at least twice a month over the past twelve years.

"Well, Scott, I accepted the partnership Joe offered me at his veterinary hospital and I found a house to rent. The entire thing needs to be cleaned, the kitchen needs to be painted and the blackberry vines are threatening to swallow the yard. I can clean and paint. No problem. But I am definitely hiring someone to fix the yard." Her eyes focused once again on the headstone. Even though the words were burned in her memory, Madeline always read them out loud.

"Scott Ryan Spencer. April 10, 1966. July 16, 1983. Racer." The word Racer was in quotes. It was her brother's nickname and also what he was.

Chapter One

Two weeks had passed since her last visit to her brother's grave. The house was now cleaned and painted and her furniture in place. Madeline had little to do but wait for Gavin Marshall to show up. He was the landscaper her friend and partner, Joe Bingham, had recommended. Since she respected Joe's advice, she had called this Marshall guy. Once her routine was established Madeline knew she could care for the yard herself, but she also knew she didn't want to.

A loud rumble filled the air around Madeline and she stepped out on the porch, blinking hard a couple of times when she saw the motorcycle stopped in her driveway. Anxiety welled in her when she saw the small child on the passenger seat.

Madeline watched the man and little boy walk toward her. The little boy's resemblance to her brother, Scott, sent chills through her entire body. Then Madeline really looked at the adult rider; suddenly she had a hard time catching her breath. In fact, she had a hard time doing anything but stare. Her eyes took in his dark hair pulled back in a ponytail, then rested for a moment on the mustache curving down over his upper lip. Madeline wondered how that mustache would feel if this man kissed her. Reluctantly, she wrenched her eyes from his face; her gaze wandered over his broad shoulders and narrow hips. A flush suffused her features as she checked out the man's tight fitting jeans, and a mental image of him standing in front of her minus everything but his hard male strength, flashed across her mind.

When she could trust herself to speak, Madeline started down the steps. She hoped the man didn't notice the glowing red spots on her cheeks.

"May I help you?" she asked, struggling to keep her

voice under control. Her insides threatened to betray the outer calm she was fighting to project.

****

Gavin swallowed hard the instant Madeline stepped out on the porch. *My God, she's beautiful.* Her dark brown hair was bound in a single braid that fell halfway down her back and although he really couldn't see her eyes, he was certain they were vivid, brown, and snapping with life. *This is a woman my mother would've approved of.* He didn't appreciate that warning bell going off and he certainly didn't welcome the desire stirring deep in the pit of his belly.

"Gavin Marshall," he said when Madeline stood mere inches from him. *I was right. Her eyes are dark, fiery brown.* "And this is Cody." Gavin indicated the little boy standing by his side. "His dad had to work overtime today so Cody's hanging out with me."

"Hi," Cody said. He was bright eyed and outgoing.

Gavin picked up on the fact Madeline seemed to shrink inside herself as soon as Cody had said hello. Why should a little boy cause this reaction in someone he had just met? *Oh, well, it doesn't matter. I'm only here to care for her yard. She won't need to see Cody again.*

****

Madeline felt her throat close up. *I'm looking at my brother all over again.* At least his name isn't Scott and he isn't Gavin's son. She didn't know why the last part should make a difference to her.

Her response to Cody was a reluctant smile and a barely audible hello. The child didn't seem to notice. Turning to Gavin she said, "Madeline Spencer." Tightness crept into her voice.

"My dad has a bird," Cody said. "It's green with a yellow patch on his head. His name is Mako. That's a shark."

"A yellow-naped Amazon," Madeline said.

"You know your birds," Gavin said.

"I've had a lot of experience treating and taking care of them," Madeline said. "Joe deals mostly with large animals and I'll be caring for the small ones, including birds. Eventually I want to set up community programs to help educate the public on birds' care and training."

"How did you become a veterinarian?" Gavin asked. "I mean, did you know for a long time that you wanted to be one?"

"Since I was six years old," Madeline said. "After I graduated from veterinary school, I worked for five years with my dad at his practice in Seattle. When he died, I kept the hospital running and then sold it a year ago."

"I assume you have animals of your own," Gavin continued.

"I don't right now," Madeline said, "but I will definitely get an animal when I'm settled in here. A cat or a dog. Maybe both."

"We're having a party at my house tonight," Cody said, all childish enthusiasm. "Do you wanna come?"

"Thank you, Cody, but I'm going to dinner at a friend's house," Madeline said. Her voice was still stiff.

"So how'd you find out about me?" Gavin asked.

"Joe recommended you and I've seen what you did with his property."

"So you've known Joe a long time?" Gavin asked.

"Since seventh grade," Madeline replied.

"Beyond the obvious, do you have any ideas on what you'd like done with the yard?"

"I don't want any bushes or vines touching the house, but I'd like some hydrangea bushes and rosebushes somewhere in the yard. I presume those used to be flower beds," Madeline continued, pointing to the crisp brown patches that undoubtedly once flourished with brilliantly colored flowers.

Gavin nodded in affirmation.

"I also want white alyssum in the flower beds. I refuse to do yard work, but I enjoy working in flower beds."

"What about a fence?" Gavin asked. "You might decide to get a dog. I could do it for you, but it would be awhile before I'd have time to do it."

"I'll let you know about the fence," Madeline said. "Right now it isn't necessary."

They stood there, the three of them, Cody showing the beginning signs of boredom.

Madeline was aware of Gavin's solid body standing way too close to her. She wanted more than anything to touch him anywhere, everywhere. She wanted to feel those sensuous lips on hers.

Somewhere in the middle of her fantasy, she heard him say her name, causing her to drop back to reality. She spun quickly around, brushing against his arm. The brief contact sent a jolt of delicious sparks through her entire body.

"Madeline?" Gavin repeated her name.

"What? I'm sorry. My mind wandered off for a minute." Madeline felt the flush sneaking back over her face.

Madeline turned to look at him.

"I just quoted you a bid of three hundred dollars," Gavin said, his voice now strangely gruff. He was watching her more closely than Madeline would have liked.

"That's fine," Madeline replied.

"You might want to call a couple of other people to see if you can get the work done for less."

"I'm not interested in getting the job done for less; I'm interested in getting it done right," Madeline said.

"Okay then. I'll be back tomorrow at one o'clock," Gavin said.

They walked back to the cycle, Cody delighted at the prospect of some action.

"How did you find this house?" Gavin asked.

"Once I accepted Joe's offer of a partnership, I came down to see it. Joe had found it and told me about it on the phone." Madeline shook her head, remembering when Joe had taken her to see the house and meet Mr. Evans, the landlord. "Joe held back more than just a little information when he told me about it."

Madeline laughed, the first sign of warmth from her. It was a pleasant sound in the late summer afternoon. "Maybe I should fence the front and back yards and start a wild animal park. It's pathetic, isn't it?"

"Nothing that can't be fixed," Gavin said.

"The house itself is structurally sound," Madeline continued. "I had that checked out, but the inside needed deep cleaning and two rooms needed painting. The one bright spot was the hardwood floors, which are in great shape."

"I asked the landlord if his seven hundred fifty dollars a month included cleaning, painting and yard work. He looked at me like he thought I was crazy and said, 'If I did all that, I'd have to get nine hundred to a thousand. Maybe more. I'm too old to do it myself and I can't afford to have it done.'"

"Then I told him I'd clean and paint and hire somebody to do the yard and give him three hundred fifty a month, signing a year's lease."

"Did he go for it?" Gavin asked.

"Not at first. Said he would be losing too much money. I told him he wouldn't be making anything at all if he didn't clean the place up."

Gavin gave a low, appreciative whistle. "You drove a hard bargain and won. I'm impressed."

"You know Mr. Evans?" Madeline asked.

"Not personally," Gavin said, "but everybody in town knows his reputation as a cheapskate. He's also one of the richest men in Heron's Cove."

Cody put on his helmet and then his leather jacket before Gavin lifted him to the passenger seat.

"You might have a hard time adjusting to this little berg," Gavin said, reaching for his own helmet.

"Do you think city dwellers lack the ability to adjust to new surroundings?" Madeline asked.

"No," Gavin said. "It's just that things are different in small towns."

"Well, I like the idea of living in Heron's Cove. Besides, I've visited Joe many times during the three years he's lived here. My favorite time was in the winter when the weather was at its stormy best. Joe and I would drive to the little cove at Heron Beach to watch the storms. I know it's a small town, but maybe that's what I need in my life right now."

****

Gavin watched Madeline for a while and wondered what else she might need. Other than his services as a landscaper he hoped it wouldn't be him. Or did he?

6

"Visiting a place isn't the same as living there," Gavin said. "You might find life annoying when you've lived here for awhile, because of the tourists and lack of big city benefits."

"Much as we hate to admit it sometimes, tourists are important to the economy, but they don't come as often as they used to," Gavin said. "When the lumber industry vanished, a good number of the town's residents and tourists vanished with it. Then sport and commercial fishing dwindled to almost nothing, and even more tourists left.

"We have festivals all year long it seems. They help some, but it's not the same as when the lumber and fishing industries were strong. Coming from the city, you'll probably find the festivals boring," Gavin said.

"Why would you say that?" Madeline asked. "As a matter of fact, Joe and I are going to the Garlic Celebration on Sunday. I'm looking forward to it. I told him I didn't have time, but that made no difference to Joe."

"Not me," Gavin said. "I've lived here all my life and seen enough of the festivals."

Gavin thought about the phone call he had gotten from Madeline Spencer, requesting a bid for his landscaping services. His interest was piqued somewhat when she said Joe Bingham had recommended him. She sounded haughty over the phone and now, after talking to her in person, Gavin was sure he didn't want anything to do with her. *Tell that to my body.* He couldn't help a second look as he and Cody rode away from Madeline's house.

He knew the important things in life were never obtained without a struggle. In fact, he savored the facets of his life that represented successful challenges. Gavin didn't know if Madeline Spencer would be important to him, but he had a sharp foreboding she would be. He did know that taking care of her lawn would be the least of the challenges he had to face where she was concerned.

****

Joe was expecting her at his house for dinner at seven o'clock and as she was getting ready, Madeline pictured her mother and Gavin Marshall meeting each other. *Well, that isn't going to happen.* If she comes down for a visit, I'll find some way to keep them apart.

Madeline also thought about Gavin Marshall. Her common sense told her to apply the brakes and stay away from him as much as possible. At the same time she felt herself falling irrevocably into his arms and his life. Madeline briefly considered hanging out with Joe or driving out to the hospital, so she wouldn't be home when Gavin came back the next day. She knew in her heart she wouldn't do either one. Although she kept telling herself she wanted to keep him out of her life, she didn't want to pass up the chance to see this man again.

Chapter Two

Joe Bingham had taken easily to life in a small town. He was beginning to feel like he had lived in Heron's Cove forever. The seeds had probably been sown early in his childhood when he used to visit his aunt and uncle on their ranch in Montana. The people in Heron's Cove were friendly and ready to lend helping hands whenever they were needed. Joe, however, had lived his entire life in Seattle and mostly felt out of place. He saw attending college, and then veterinary school, in Pullman, Washington as his salvation from the craziness of big city life.

Joe had lived in Heron's Cove for three years, but in less than a year the people had accepted him and trusted his care of their animals. He had a ten-acre place, which was ideal for a horse, so before his first year was up, he had purchased a Quarter Horse mare. Much of his free time was spent riding which meant Joe couldn't be bothered with caring for a yard either.

The little town had been good for him and to him, and now Joe hoped Heron's Cove would work its magic for Madeline, too.

He worked in his kitchen, putting the finishing touches on the meal he planned to serve Madeline tonight. Soon they would be dining on grilled steaks, baked potatoes with all the trimmings and salad. Joe knew she would relish banana splits for dessert, so the fixings for those were waiting in the fridge. For just himself, Joe didn't usually bother much with cooking, relying on take-out meals, but having company provided good reason to dust off his interest in the culinary arts.

Joe understood he and Madeline had been friends, almost like brother and sister, far too long for there to be a possibility of a more serious relationship, but still he was pleased to have her here and he looked forward to working with her. Madeline's warmth and sense of humor would go a long way to putting the human clients at ease when they brought their animals to the hospital. They had kept in touch through the years, so when he knew it was time to take on a partner in the hospital, Madeline was the only person he thought of approaching.

As the lone veterinarian in Heron's Cove, Joe had been given the task of treating small animals as well as the large ones, which were his area of expertise. There had been times when he came close to buckling under the workload, so having a partner in the hospital would work well for him and the community, especially a person he knew as well as he did Madeline.

****

On the drive out to Joe's place, Madeline couldn't find any reason to feel depressed. The weather was at its stunning best, with clear blue skies and daytime temperatures in the eighties. Even now, at five o'clock in the afternoon, it was still warm enough for Madeline to wear a tank top, shorts and sandals. Everywhere she looked on the drive out, she saw flowers in bloom so she rolled down the windows of her car to better take in the scents of the summer evening.

Madeline stopped her car in Joe's driveway. He came out to meet her with his arms open wide.

"Hey, Maddy," Joe said in familiar greeting.

They exchanged hugs, then Madeline stepped back and said, "I can't get over how gorgeous your yard is." She chuckled softly. "It's like driving through a park."

"What's so funny?" Joe asked.

"You are so much like me when it comes to doing yard work. Or should I say not doing it?"

Joe shook his head from side to side. "Why do you suppose we turned out like this? We aren't lazy people."

"I don't know about you, but I know how I ended up hating yard work. It's because Mom and Dad had Scott and me mow and rake as part of our regular chores."

"Scott hated it more than you did, didn't he?" Joe asked.

"Oh God, yes. He used to pitch the worst kind of fits

10

whenever he had to work in the yard. He hated doing most anything that took him away from racing his bike."

Madeline looked around at the rosebushes, the precisely edged sidewalk and the velvety smooth grass. If this was an example of the work Gavin Marshall did, Joe had been right to recommend him. Madeline still wondered, though, if she had been right to hire him since her first sight of him had caused such upheaval in the core of her being.

With Gavin working as her landscaper, Madeline knew she would be seeing more of motorcycles, and Gavin, than she would be comfortable with. She could hire someone else to care for her yard which would remove the discomfort, but she just wasn't sure she wanted to do that.

Madeline was determined to enjoy herself. She knew Joe was trying to make her feel welcome and she appreciated the effort she knew he'd made. He had found the house for her and offered her a chance to work at a dream job. Madeline knew his efforts wouldn't stop at the job offer, but that Joe would be there for her no matter what. She would do no less for him, and she knew part of that included not living in her past.

When they were seated around the table on the back deck of Joe's house, sipping pre-dinner drinks, Madeline broached the subject of Gavin Marshall. She wished to clear the air before the evening started.

"Joe," she began, "why did you suggest I contact Gavin Marshall for the landscaping job? You know how I feel about motorcycles."

Joe held up his hand, signaling for silence.

"Broken hearts have a way of healing, Maddy. Yours will, too, if you give it a chance." He took her hand in his. "What happened is in the past. Yes, it was tragic, but dwelling on it isn't going to change anything and it won't make your life better. I'm not telling you to forget, Maddy; that wouldn't be right. But you need to let your life continue.

"As for Gavin Marshall, I hired him for only one reason, and I recommended him to you for the same reason. He's good at what he does. The fact he rides a motorcycle has nothing to do with how he does his job.

Three people independently recommended Gavin to me after I had trouble with my first two landscapers. You've driven by that house on the corner of 14th and Heron?"

Madeline nodded.

"Gavin Marshall. That place belongs to a retired judge and his wife. Gavin designed the entire project himself. That really cemented his standing as a first-class landscaper. Now, I think it's time for us to embrace life in the present."

Madeline hated to admit it, but she knew Joe was right. It was doubtful she would change his mind on the subjects of Gavin Marshall or motorcycles, and he certainly wouldn't change hers.

"You're right, Joe," she said. "Let's eat." She went inside to help him carry the food outside.

Joe started laughing, nearly spilling his drink.

"What's so funny?" Madeline asked.

"I was just thinking about your adjustment to living in a small town like this. Face it, Maddy, you lived in Seattle your entire life except for the three years at vet school."

"What's so humorous about that?" Madeline asked, a touch of irritation crawling into her voice.

"You enjoy all the conveniences and possibilities a big city offers, Maddy. You'll have to do without most of those in Heron's Cove. I know you've been down here to visit, but there is a big difference between visiting a place and actually living there."

"Gavin said the same things this afternoon," Madeline said. "I think I'm smart enough to realize that. Plus if I want to do some major shopping or go to a concert or something, I can drive to Seattle or Portland."

Joe wisely steered the conversation away from Madeline's adjustment to life in Heron's Cove.

"Things have been pretty quiet around here so maybe we can enjoy our meal without being bothered by the phone ringing," Joe said. "In fact I'm so confident the phone won't ring that I left my pager and cell phone inside."

"Is Janice coming for dinner tonight?" Madeline asked.

"No," Joe said. "We're not seeing each other anymore."

"I'm sorry, Joe."

"Don't be. Some things aren't meant to be and this was one of them."

Despite Joe's confidence that their dinner wouldn't be disturbed, the phone rang halfway through dinner. With a rueful look at Madeline, Joe got up to answer it.

"Hey, what's up?" Madeline heard him ask. "Yes, she is. Just a minute."

Madeline wasn't annoyed by the interruption, rather she was reminded of one of the reasons she moved to Heron's Cove. Taking care of animals was something she knew and loved, and if this call meant she had to go in to the hospital to help in an emergency, she was prepared to do it.

Joe came back out, smiling apologetically.

"It's Gavin," he said. "He's at a friend's house and the guy's parrot escaped. Will you talk to him?"

"Of course I will," Madeline said, getting up immediately.

Joe went back to the table and watched Madeline go inside.

"What happened?" she asked, after picking up the phone.

"I'm at a friend's house for the party Cody invited you to. I was grilling on the back deck and I forgot to close the sliding screen door. Something spooked the bird and he flew out."

This admission told Madeline she didn't need to ask if the bird's wings were clipped, and it seemed a replay of a number of stories she had heard before. People ignored the importance of clipping their birds' wings, thinking the process would hurt the birds. It didn't. Or, they believed birds were meant to fly. They were. In the wild. But in domestic life, there were too many dangers lurking for a bird that escaped.

"How many people are there?" she asked.

"Eight. Dennis, he's the one who owns the bird, and another guy went out to look for the bird."

"Okay. Did they drive?"

"No," Gavin said.

"Good. Tell just one other person to go out and get them. No calling their names or anything. He just needs to walk at a normal pace until he finds them."

"Okay." Gavin's voice became muffled and Madeline could hear him talking to someone.

She heard a door slam.

"Madeline? They just came back. No sign of the bird. Now what?"

"Let me talk to Dennis," Madeline said. She heard background party noise while she waited for Gavin's friend to pick up the phone.

"Dennis? I'm Madeline Spencer. Your bird's name is Mako, right?"

"Yeah. He's a yellow-naped Amazon."

"Can you get Mako's cage out on the back deck?" Madeline asked.

"Sure."

"Okay, do that and leave the cage door open. You can watch for Mako. Also go out on the deck, maybe every half hour, and call his name. Don't shout. Go on with what you were doing, just keep the volume down."

"Mako comes to a whistle I made up," Dennis offered and Madeline sensed the hope in his voice.

"That's even better," Madeline said. "Do that and you can call his name, too, if you want."

"Thanks," Dennis said. "What do I owe you?"

"Nothing, except the promise you'll get Mako's wings clipped."

"Deal," Dennis said.

Joe returned to the kitchen carrying Madeline's unfinished dinner. He covered the plate with tin foil and put it in the oven to keep it warm. Then he listened with rapt attention even though he could only hear Madeline's side of the conversation.

"Does Mako have a favorite snack or treat?" Madeline asked, speaking to Dennis again.

"Yeah, he loves peanuts. Every night, about this time, I give him some."

Madeline breathed a sigh of relief. "That's good. Okay, put the peanuts in the feed cup. And, Dennis?"

"Yes?"

"Our deal. As soon as possible after Mako comes home, bring him into Joe's office and I'll clip his wings. It will be better for him and for you."

"Won't it hurt him?"

"Absolutely not. I will only cut his flight feathers enough so he can't make another escape like he did tonight. When you bring Mako in, I'll show you a diagram of a bird's wing so you'll know just which feathers I will be clipping."

"Okay, I'll be there. Uh, Gavin wants to talk to you again."

When Gavin had picked up the phone again, Madeline said, "Do me a favor, please."

"Name it."

"Call me just as soon as Mako comes back. I don't care what time it is."

When she hung up the phone, Madeline got a round of applause from her eavesdropper.

"You were awesome, Maddy, but then I knew you would be. I'm sorry your dinner was interrupted," Joe said, removing the foil-covered plate from the oven.

"That's okay," Madeline said, and she meant it. "It's the reason I'm here."

She finished her dinner without further interruption, and then helped Joe make the banana splits.

"Do you think the bird will come back?" Joe asked later, as he and Madeline cleared away the dishes.

"Well," Madeline began thoughtfully, "there's a good chance he will. Most creatures feel a strong attachment to their home and they try hard to return there."

"If he had to fly away, this was a good time for it to happen weather-wise. Even if he was out all night, it won't get too cold for him since Amazon parrots can tolerate fairly cold temperatures. There's a chance some critter could get him, though. I didn't want to say it to Dennis or to Gavin,, but I'm sure they probably realize that."

Madeline stopped to take a bite of her dinner, "I told him to bring Mako in when he came back, so I could clip his wings."

"Will you need help?" Joe asked.

"I shouldn't," Madeline said. "Dennis said Mako is really tame and used to being handled, especially by him. I figure he can hold his wings out, one at a time, and I can clip."

****

Madeline was keyed up and felt like driving around awhile before she went home. She knew she couldn't since she wanted to be by the phone in case Gavin called about his friend's bird.

She had a couple of other issues she knew would keep her from getting a good night's sleep. Tomorrow afternoon at four o'clock a reporter from the Weekly Monitor was coming by to interview her. She hadn't been at all surprised when the newspaper contacted her shortly after she got to Heron's Cove. News of Madeline's pending arrival in town had already spread through the little community like a fire in the dune grass. The newspaper apparently wanted to make her arrival official by way of an article and pictures.

Before the reporter was scheduled to stop by, Gavin Marshall would be there to start on the yard and that caused Madeline great concern. She considered not being home when he got there. After all, Gavin didn't need to come in the house for anything and she could send his check to the address on the business card he'd left with her. Madeline knew she could probably hang out with Joe or spend the time at the hospital while Gavin was working. However, she wasn't crazy about passing up a chance to be near the man who caused such chaos in the innermost parts of her.

Madeline suddenly remembered Joe had only lived in Heron's Cove for three years. If she knew anything at all about yard upkeep, she knew it took longer than three growing seasons for a yard to look as good as Joe's did. That meant a couple of things.

More than likely the landscaping was well established when Joe bought the place. If that was true, then maybe Gavin Marshall wasn't such a genius after all when it came to landscaping. The work had already been done and all he had to do was maintain it. That thought perked up Madeline's spirits since she now figured she could hire someone else. In reality, Madeline knew it was too late for that because deep down she didn't *want* to hire somebody else.

By the time she had sorted through these matters, Madeline had pulled up in her driveway determined to stay awake waiting for the phone call from Gavin.

Walking into her house, Madeline felt a little lonely and said out loud, "Maybe I should get a dog."

Willing herself to stay awake, Madeline sat scrunched up in her old, gray recliner going over the events of the past couple days. She hadn't been willing to leave the chair behind, or get rid of it as her mother suggested. The chair had been with her through college and was like an old friend.

She picked up the novel she was reading, but abandoned that when the words started melting together on the page. Even though she was tense and thought sleep would forsake her, Madeline's eyelids eventually became too heavy to stay open. When she finally did sleep, it was only to be disturbed by images of flying motorcycles and talking horses. At least the nightmare about Scott left her alone this night.

Chapter Three

It was nearly midnight when an insistent ringing pulled Madeline from her fitful dozing in the recliner. When she realized it was the phone, she made an effort to uncurl her body. Her attempt to work the kink out of her neck wasn't successful, as she walked to the kitchen on sleep-stiffened legs, still rubbing her neck.

"Hello?" Madeline struggled to hold the receiver to her ear.

"Madeline? It's Gavin. Mako landed on his perch about ten minutes ago. He's just fine, but he was definitely anxious to get back in his cage. Do you still want Dennis to bring him in tomorrow?"

"Absolutely. The sooner I can clip Mako's wings, the better off he will be. Tell Dennis to be there at nine tomorrow morning."

"Will do. Thanks you again, Madeline...for everything."

Madeline crawled into bed after the phone call and when she fell asleep, she was agitated by the recurring nightmare of the accident. She never knew for sure when the ghastly images would hold peaceful sleep at bay. Madeline had tried over the counter and prescription sleeping medication in the past, but neither had any effect on the dreams.

When she woke up at eight fifteen, she felt as though she hadn't slept all night. She hated having to rush through her morning, preferring a leisurely breakfast outside when the weather was as beautiful as it had been for the past couple of weeks. Eating would be delayed, however.

In her sleep-deprived state, it took Madeline several minutes to realize Gavin would be coming by to take care of the yard later today. Madeline fixed that all-important

18

cup of morning coffee. *Great, that man is one distraction I don't need in my life. Now or ever.*

Even though he was a distraction to her personally, her lawn was in desperate need. She did have to admit Joe's yard was impressive even if Gavin hadn't done the original landscaping. She had to wonder how much time he would have to spend at her house. She didn't know if she was up for seeing his motorcycle sitting out front every time he came over. *Oh well, he can't bring his yard work equipment on his motorcycle.* Surely someone else in Heron's Cove, someone who didn't ride a cycle, could do the job as well. Okay, maybe not as well, but good enough to suit her.

Madeline added cream to her coffee and slipped outside to stand on the front porch. She had told Dennis to be at the hospital at nine o'clock and it was already eight thirty. Madeline took a couple swigs of her coffee, and then hurried off to shower and dress. She was hungry, but resigned herself to having breakfast when she returned home.

****

Joe was already at the hospital when Madeline arrived. She had asked him to be there in case she needed someone to hold the bird after all. Madeline noticed he had brought a box of doughnuts.

"Joseph Bingham, you know those really aren't a healthy food item," she said, gesturing toward the box.

"Maddy, you're such a hypocrite." Joe took a huge bite out of a jelly filled doughnut. "You know perfectly well you'll have one when we're finished with the bird."

Dennis arrived right on time, carrying Mako in a portable cage. Cody followed his dad closely.

Joe's help hadn't been required, but he stayed to watch the entire wing clipping process.

"Why do you clip the flight feathers?" he asked.

"Those are the only feathers a bird doesn't lose to the molting process," Madeline answered. "They have to be clipped for the safety of the bird because when the flight feathers are clipped properly and a bird escapes, it won't be able to fly away like Mako did."

"Maddy, I'm really impressed by how you handle

19

birds," Joe said, as they were closing up the hospital later that day.

"You saw how easy it was to clip Mako's wings. He's been well-socialized which made my job that much easier."

"You know I would've helped, but I'm glad you and Dennis had the situation under control. Those huge beaks terrify me."

"I've been bit more times than I want to remember," Madeline said, "and the beaks scared me at first, too. A lot of it is in how you approach a bird initially. Stick with me, Joe. I'll make you a bird doctor yet."

Finished with her job at the hospital, Madeline headed for home wishing she had gone horseback riding on the beach with Joe.

Home. Madeline wasn't entirely sure she wanted to call Heron's Cove home yet. Maybe that's why she was only leasing the house she was living in. She figured the year's lease period gave her an easy escape if things didn't work out here. Madeline seriously considered buying the house she was in if she decided to stay in Heron's Cove permanently. It had everything she was looking for.

Although some areas of Madeline's life had sometimes lacked direction, her career path was set early on. She knew from the time she was a small child she wanted to be a veterinarian and she never swayed from that initial decision. Part of her career planning included joining her father in his practice when she graduated from veterinary school. Madeline had done this.

Would Scott have joined us? Probably not, since he didn't share his family's interest in and love for animals. His focus never strayed from anything related to motorcycles. Especially racing. *No, I can't let myself think about Scott. Not now. I'm not ready. Maybe I'll never be ready.*

The practice was left to Madeline when her father passed away and for a time afterwards she kept it in operation. Her mother still lived in Seattle, but Madeline saw little reason to stay in the city where she'd spent most of her life. The memories were just too strong there.

Her father's death left Madeline with an enormous

void in her life. She wished she could have talked to him about Scott, about her feelings of blame even though she knew he hadn't held her responsible. *So why can't I see the circumstances the way he did,* Madeline's thoughts of her brother once again overtook her consciousness.

Shaking her head in yet another attempt to dispel the agitation from her mind, Madeline remembered to be grateful her father had left her financially comfortable, if not wealthy. Part of the agreement had been that if the practice were sold, the proceeds would be divided equally between Madeline and her mother. Madeline's share of the money from the sale of the veterinary practice in North Seattle provided enough money to buy into Joe's practice and enough money for a down payment on a house, if she decided to stay in Heron's Cove.

The memories of her brother weren't the only reason Madeline wanted to get away from Seattle. She recalled her final conversation with her ex-fiancée, Allen, during which he'd broken their engagement.

"I'm sorry, Madeline, so sorry, but it has to be over between us. You're obsessed with Scott's death." She could still hear him saying these words, almost as if he were sitting beside her again.

When she'd started to protest, Allen signaled for silence. "No, Madeline. I've heard all your arguments before and hearing them one more time isn't going to change my mind. I could be happy with you, but I can't live with the ghost of a man you'll probably never let me measure up to."

Madeline had jerked the ring off her finger and thrown it at Allen, not waiting to see if he picked it up. She ran to her bedroom and slammed the door, throwing herself on the bed. Hours later when she stopped crying, Madeline went back to the living room. The ring was gone.

"First Scott, then Dad. Now Allen. Every man in my life that I've been close to has left me. Well, Madeline Spencer, it isn't going to happen again." She choked back one last sob.

Then, just six months ago, Joe had called. At the end of a very long conversation, he told Madeline his plan for the future, and she felt like a floundering swimmer who had just been tossed a life ring.

Joe started with his plan almost like he thought he was going to have to work to convince her. "Maddy, I think it's time I took on a partner at the hospital. There are a lot of exotic birds here and I don't know enough to treat them. You're the only person I thought of asking."

"Joe, I couldn't possibly give you an answer about the partnership now. My life is in just too much of an upheaval. But I will definitely come to Heron's Cove and work with you at the hospital if that's acceptable."

"I'm ecstatic you're coming down here," Joe said. "Your expertise, especially with birds, will be so welcome. Take all the time you need to make up your mind about the partnership. I mean that."

Madeline glanced at her watch as she pulled into her driveway and finished reminiscing. It was only ten o'clock, just an hour since she'd gone to the hospital to take care of Mako. She checked her answering machine and saw she had one message waiting. Maybe Gavin had called to cancel. She punched the button and listened to the nasal voice. "Ms. Spencer, this is Marla from National Mortgage Company. I'm surprised you haven't called me back. I can offer..." Madeline hung up. *Great—the telemarketers have found me again.*

****

Across town Gavin Marshall checked on the time, too. "God damn it!" The cursing gave him no satisfaction and released none of the tension filling him. He knew it was far too early to go over to Madeline's house.

Gavin paced his small kitchen like some crazed circus animal until he came to a decision. He'd wait an hour, if he could, and then call. He even rehearsed out loud what he would say. "Dr. Spencer, this is Gavin Marshall. My other job got cancelled so I can do your yard earlier, if that's okay."

Until he saw Madeline again only one thing could provide gratification and that was his motorcycle. He picked up his helmet, grabbed his leather jacket from the hook by the back door and headed for the garage. That bike was his pride and joy and just looking at her now drained away some of the stress he was experiencing.

Picturing Madeline on a bike, especially on a bike with him, brought a whole new set of images to Gavin's mind and the sudden heat of desire flashed deep inside his loins. He could feel her arms wrapped around his waist and feel her breasts pressed into his back. Not surprisingly, he found himself riding down the street that ran by her house. There was no doubt in his mind, he wanted her.

Gavin regained his senses just before he turned into Madeline's driveway. He knew it wouldn't do any good to show up on his bike. Madeline would fire him before he even had a chance to start work. Hopefully she hadn't seen him. Gavin didn't want Madeline to think he was stalking her. He rode home without slowing down, but his thoughts were a little slower to catch up. They lingered for a time at Madeline's house.

****

The rumble of a motorcycle jolted Madeline sharply back to the present. *It has to be Gavin.* Filled with anticipation, she hurried to the living room to look out the window. Only the sight of a motorcycle disappearing up the street rewarded her gaze. Madeline couldn't be sure it was Gavin. Disappointment washed over her like water released from a dam.

Madeline had grown up around bikes, starting to ride dirt bikes when she was just seven years old. She worked and saved her money. When she was seventeen and with lots of advice from her parents, she had purchased her own motorcycle. She recalled how nervous and excited she had been on her first solo ride, traveling from their house in north Seattle to Southcenter Mall and back. She also recalled exactly how pumped that ride made her feel.

She remembered riding together as a family. She didn't know if her mother was still riding motorcycles. If she still rode, she didn't say anything about it to Madeline. However, Madeline would bet almost anything her mother had kept her motorcycle endorsement all these years. She loved riding too much to give it up. Madeline chuckled when she thought about Gavin meeting her mother. Madeline couldn't believe she just put Gavin and her mother in the same thought. If it came right down to it, they actually had quite a bit in common but, if Madeline had anything to say about it, they would never meet.

As Madeline began to remove her mother from the picture, her throat became dry as she pictured herself riding behind Gavin. Her pulse raced as they started on that imaginary ride. Her arms enfolded him as they cruised down the road, her head rested lightly against his broad back. After the ride, they would stop somewhere for dinner and when he brought her home Madeline would invite him in and they would... Madeline shook her head from side to side, ending the journey they had just been on. She knew it was dangerous to let her thoughts continue in this vein.

Madeline found herself at loose ends and she didn't like it. It gave her too much time to think. She couldn't bear all the thoughts she had of Gavin Marshall.

****

True to his word, Gavin showed up just before one o'clock, driving a late model blue truck. A trailer holding a riding lawnmower was hooked to the truck. She didn't see them, but Madeline assumed Gavin had also brought other tools.

She struggled over whether to go outside and talk to him or just let him get on with his work. Meanwhile, she watched him from the living room window. Oh, how she watched him. Gavin wore a white T-shirt with the sleeves cut off, setting off his deep tan and broad, solid shoulders. His hair was bound neatly in a braid this time, a bandana tied around his head. As determined as she was to distance herself from this man, Madeline couldn't possible ignore those tight fitting jeans. Her pulse raced as she contemplated what the jeans were covering. She was glad Gavin couldn't see her right now.

Madeline made a decision. She went to the kitchen for a drink of water and tried to collect herself. Then she stepped outside.

****

"Gavin."

Gavin looked up from the lawnmower he was

unloading. The sight of Madeline standing there in a sleeveless, summer dress, her long hair wound into a bun at the base of her neck, made him feel as though someone had slugged him in the pit of his stomach. He swallowed hard before he spoke. He knew he had to say something soon or he'd rush up on the porch and pull Madeline to him, crushing her lips with kiss after kiss before he carried her into the house.

"I wasn't sure you'd talk to a ruffian like me." He thought he could cover his unease by keeping the tone of his conversation flip. There was nothing he could do to disguise his desire. Gavin felt the swelling pushing against the constraint of his jeans. "Or do you intend to stay outside to make sure I do what you hired me for? You could help me if you wanted to. That way I could get done faster and..." Gavin deliberately let his voice trail off, enjoying the flush creeping over Madeline's face.

"I came out to tell you I made a pitcher of lemonade so if you get thirsty or if you need anything..." Madeline, her eyes downcast and her voice low, let the remainder of her sentence fade away. The flush was even more apparent in her cheeks now. "Just be sure to knock first."

"I brought water, but lemonade sounds a lot better. Thanks." Gavin busied himself once again to hide his shock and pleasure at Madeline's offer. Wondering if it had really been an invitation, he managed to get the lawnmower unloaded. Drinking lemonade was the furthest thing from Gavin Marshall's mind, but now he had a reason for knocking on Madeline's door.

****

Madeline wondered what she could have been thinking, inviting this man into her house. She didn't want to admit, even to herself, what drove her to say those words. She tried unsuccessfully to convince herself she hadn't actually invited him, that she had merely extended a polite offer.

The day was still young, but Madeline's nerves felt as frayed as old wiring. Too late she wished she had suggested the interview take place at the hospital. She wanted to stay home, but at the same time she wanted to be gone while Gavin Marshall worked in the yard.

Madeline was having difficulty remembering when she had ever been this indecisive. Sure, she had made bad decisions before, but at least she'd made them without this much vacillation. She hated this part of herself, but she didn't seem to be able to control it where Gavin Marshall was concerned. She was acting like a girl in the grasp of her first crush. She couldn't remember blushing as much as she had in the past couple of days.

Although it made her jump, the jangling telephone provided a welcome distraction just then and Madeline rushed to answer it. The diversion was a short one, however, since it was a wrong number.

Madeline looked forward to attending the Garlic Festival tomorrow. According to the weather report, clear skies and sunshine were in the forecast. Joe had the ability to make most occasions fun, so Madeline was counting on a few hours when she didn't have to talk to or think about Gavin.

Chapter Four

Madeline wondered if she could find respite if she settled down to read the novel she had recently started. At least she might be able to lose herself in the intricacies of the whodunit puzzle. She read a lot of mystery novels and this book was the second one in a series by her favorite author. When she had tried to read last night waiting up for Gavin to call, she found the words on the page blending one into the other. Now as she sat holding the book in her hands, the words didn't make any sense to Madeline. She tossed the book aside, losing her place in the process. She didn't think she'd have better luck reading some of her professional journals, but decided to give it a try.

Since she had time on her hands, and nothing pressing requiring her attention, Madeline did pull out some veterinary journals so she could catch up on reading them. She found it hard to concentrate on what should have been routine material. Her thoughts and desires kept skipping around outside with Gavin as he tended to the yard.

Madeline finally waded through one complete article and half of another one before a light tapping on the kitchen door distracted her.

She was intoxicated by the heady scent of sweat mingled with raw male musk the minute she opened the door. Gavin Marshall stood there, leaning casually against the doorjamb.

"Can I use the bathroom?" he asked, his green eyes burning into Madeline's face.

"Of course. Down the hall, second door on the left." Madeline gestured to accompany her directions, thankful her voice didn't betray the storm churning through her insides. Her heart beat so loudly in her ears she was certain anyone around her could hear. *My God, Gavin is actually in my house.* She berated herself for letting him in, and then set about gathering the journals she had been trying so hard to read while Gavin worked in the yard.

Intent as she was on the turmoil raging inside her, she was unaware Gavin had returned and was now standing just inches from her position at the kitchen table. Madeline dropped her hands to her sides when he spoke.

"Madeline? Thanks." Gavin's voice crashed like thunder in the confines of the small kitchen.

She turned around to face him. The magazines she had been holding slid unnoticed from her hand and fell to the floor.

Gavin reached for Madeline, then quickly let his hands fall to his sides.

Madeline felt strangely disappointed when Gavin didn't kiss her. She wanted his kiss, his touch, but she just stood there and watched him go out the back door.

Madeline glanced at the clock on the kitchen wall, remembering a reporter from the *Weekly Monitor* was coming at four o'clock to interview her. She had a half hour to forget all about the kiss that almost happened. Madeline knew she couldn't afford to give in to the feelings he so easily aroused in her. No, she would be better off forgetting all about Gavin Marshall. Sooner, rather than later.

At five minutes before four, an energetic tapping on Madeline's door announced the arrival of the reporter.

"Dr. Spencer?" she asked.

"Yes, but please call me Madeline. Dr. Spencer makes me sound like my father."

"Okay, I'm Robin Davis," she offered her hand to Madeline.

After Robin declined anything to eat or drink, the two women sat down in the living room. They exchanged small talk for a few minutes prior to starting the interview.

"Were both your parents veterinarians?" Robin asked.

"No," Madeline answered. "My mother was a nurse but she's retired now and enjoying her second childhood. Sometimes, I think she has more energy than I do. Wait a minute. I know she does." Madeline laughed.

"It sounds like you're very close to your mother."

Madeline paused before responding to this. "Yes, I am. We have strong differences, of course, which I think is part of the mother-daughter package. I can truly say, though, that my mother is my friend. She's kept me grounded all these years, and at times it hasn't been easy for her."

"When did you decide you wanted to be a veterinarian?"

"I think I was about six years old. Naturally, I was aware of the work both my parents did, but my dad's work fascinated me. I especially loved it when he let me go with him to the hospital."

"You said your mom was a nurse. Did you ever consider that as a career choice?"

"No," Madeline answered, without hesitation. "It wasn't that I didn't appreciate what she did helping sick people, but I wanted to help sick and injured animals. Animals have been a part of my life ever since I can remember."

Robin looked around the room. "You must have pets of your own."

Why do people take for granted I have pets just because I'm a vet? "No, I don't. Maybe I will when I'm more settled in my job here."

"You're a bird specialist, right?" Robin asked.

"I'm not a specialist," Madeline replied, "but I have a lot of experience treating birds."

"Do you have any particular message for pet owners in Heron's Cove?"

"I would definitely encourage people to have their cats and dogs spayed or neutered. The hospital offers a low-cost program to lighten the burden somewhat for those on fixed incomes."

Madeline continued when she saw she truly had Robin's attention. "One of the things I'd like to do in the near future is to offer classes on bird care. I'm also hoping to start a visitation program where people can bring animals, properly socialized and certified healthy, to visit nursing home residents."

Robin changed the track of the interview and for the first time Madeline felt uncomfortable.

"I understand you ride motorcycles. Would you like to talk a little about that?"

Madeline swallowed hard a couple of times. This reporter had definitely done her homework, which probably included talking to Joe. Madeline knew she had to answer, but she wasn't about to go into great detail.

"There isn't much to tell," Madeline said stiffly. "I rode a long time ago, but not any more."

"That's okay," Robin said. "I don't have to mention motorcycles in the article. It's all about introducing you as the newest veterinarian in Heron's Cove."

After nearly an hour and a half, Madeline was finally by herself, sitting on the front porch enjoying the warm afternoon. The interview had been enjoyable overall, especially since it freed Madeline from thinking about Gavin. The reporter asked intelligent questions and seemed genuinely interested in getting to know Madeline.

Madeline's thoughts returned to Gavin. She couldn't believe she had agreed to pay him three hundred dollars for his afternoon's work. At the same time, Madeline marveled at how the lawn had been transformed from a weed patch to neatly clipped grass. Gone, too, were the blackberry vines. The flower beds had been cleaned out, ready for further manipulation. Madeline knew she would enjoy working with these, maybe planting some bulbs in the fall. She didn't consider tinkering in flower beds to be yard work, which she hated to do. No, this would be an opportunity for artistic expression. With Gavin Marshall still pressing on her thoughts Madeline got up and walked inside.

It wasn't until she was in bed, almost asleep, that Madeline realized Gavin had left this afternoon without his payment. She wondered if it would seem cowardly to mail him a check. If she did, it would be one less time she had to be near him. That made up her mind; she wouldn't be mailing any check to Gavin.

****

The article about Madeline wouldn't be out until Wednesday, but after church, she was surrounded by people alternately welcoming her to Heron's Cove and asking her questions about their animals. The small town information pipeline was alive and well.

Madeline could see it coming that folks would soon be asking her to take in unwanted pets while she silently hoped no one would simply drop animals off in her yard.

She excused herself from one conversation, but before she got to her car, she was wrapped up in talking to a lady about her indecision over adopting a dog from the shelter.

"My daughter raises pure-bred miniature Schnauzers and I could get a puppy from her. That would be a known quantity, but a dog from the shelter...well...I just don't know."

"There are some wonderful dogs and a few puppies," Madeline told the woman. "They're all in desperate need of good homes. If you'd like, I'll meet you at the shelter tomorrow, at your convenience, and we can look at the dogs together."

"Thank you, Dr. Spencer," the woman said. "Tomorrow at one o'clock would be perfect for me."

"It's agreed then," Madeline said. "I'll meet you at the shelter at one."

Finally making her good-byes for the morning, Madeline walked across the street to her car. She wasn't worried about being late for her afternoon with Joe. He was picking her up at one and it was only eleven thirty now.

While she waited at home, she freshened up and changed clothes before she sat down to watch television. Madeline wished she had taken time for coffee and cookies after church today because she was getting rather hungry. She knew they would be eating at the festival, but still it was hard not to fix something for lunch.

"Joe, you look like a tourist," Madeline said when he came by to pick her up. He wore a T-shirt, shorts and sandals, but it was the hat and dark glasses that really stood out.

"Well, Miss Madeline, today I am a tourist and so shall you be." Joe bowed to Madeline in the manner of a court jester.

"Joseph Bingham, you are way too much, and I'm not sure I should even be seen in your company."

"It's too late, my dear. You're stuck with me." Joe offered Madeline his arm.

Madeline laughed as she picked up her purse and they headed out the door.

She was glad the weather was at its spectacular best. While she didn't mind the rain, she realized it was always better to have good weather for outdoor festivities. Rain probably wouldn't have prevented Madeline from attending. She had learned long ago that if she let the northwest rain keep her housebound, she would never go anywhere.

Joe acted like an eager child once they got to the festival grounds, barely giving Madeline time to examine the items at one booth before dragging her along to the next one. Joe lingered at the booths with garlic products as his main interest was in sampling.

"Hey, Maddy, you have to try the garlic-flavored ice cream."

"No, I don't," Madeline wrinkled her nose.

Joe ignored her, "It's great. Trust me on this one."

"Joe, I think you missed your calling," Madeline said, accepting a spoonful of garlic ice cream from the young girl at the booth. "You should have been a chef."

"I have actually been thinking about opening a restaurant," Joe said thoughtfully. "I don't suppose you'd..." He let his words fade.

Madeline cast a look at her friend as if he had lost his mind.

"Joe, you've got to be kidding. What about your practice? Surely you wouldn't give that up."

"No," Joe said, "I wouldn't. That definitely comes first. I was thinking I could open just a small place and hire people to run it for me."

"You'd better think about the idea some more," Madeline said. "A *whole* lot more. You might also want to get out of the sun for a while. I think it's affecting your mind."

It seemed Joe knew everyone in Heron's Cove and soon the two of them were part of a group of a dozen people walking around the festival grounds. Joe dropped the subject of the restaurant for the time being while the group continued visiting the booths, several of them more than once. They sat down to eat lunch, listening to the band entertaining the crowd, delighting in the dancing efforts of grown-ups and children.

"Come on, Maddy," Joe said, taking her hand and pulling her to her feet. "Let's dance."

When Joe and Madeline were in junior-high school, Madeline and Joe's parents had insisted they both learn to dance. They had both shown real talent and it was something they still loved to do. Tonight, they drew enthusiastic applause for their efforts, and after several minutes, sat down, out of breath.

Joe and Madeline had been at the festival for a couple of hours when Madeline spotted Gavin in the crowd. She tried unsuccessfully to steer Joe in the opposite direction, but his attention was firmly riveted on a booth selling leather hats and coats. Gavin spotted them and came striding over.

"Hey, Joe, how's it going?" Gavin and Joe exchanged that complicated, secret handshake so common among close friends.

Gavin looked at Madeline and smiled.

"Madeline. Good to see you again." His easy tone did nothing to settle the unrest Madeline felt.

She nodded in acknowledgement of his greeting. "I thought you weren't going to any more local festivals."

"Yeah, well, I got coerced into going by Dennis and Cody. They're here someplace." Gavin looked around, trying to spot his friends.

"You forgot to pick up your money yesterday," Madeline said. "Do you want me to mail you a check?"

"No. If I don't come by tonight to pick it up, I'll get it the next time I do your yard." Gavin winked at Madeline and walked off.

Madeline couldn't believe it. She glared at Joe and said nothing to Gavin's retreating form.

It was nearly six o'clock when Joe dropped Madeline off at her house. He was going home to pour over his prized acquisition, a garlic cookbook compiled by local chefs. Madeline planned to read for a while before heading to bed.

However, once she was alone, Madeline gave up trying to banish thoughts of Gavin from her mind. She didn't want them to, but the thoughts swept over and around her, making her dizzy with a mixture of desire and dread. Why was this man taunting her and why was she letting him? Madeline just wanted him to go away. Or did she?

****

After he had seen Madeline at the festival, Gavin lost most of his enthusiasm for continuing the ride he had started with Dennis and Cody. He only wanted to be near her, holding her, kissing her. Oh, how he wanted to take it further than the holding and kissing, but he didn't want to rush Madeline in any way. She would have to want him, too, at least in small measure.

Since this outing had been planned for a long time, Gavin didn't want to disappoint Cody. So he caught up with Cody and his dad.

Gavin was troubled by Madeline's attitude toward him and toward motorcycles in general. He'd ridden bikes for most of his life and had never been involved in an accident. The only bump on his record was a speeding ticket he had received a few years back. He always wore the proper equipment when he rode, and if he carried a passenger, he made sure that person was dressed as well as or better than himself.

As he considered her feelings and realized he couldn't get her off of his mind, he was afraid he might be developing feelings for Madeline. More than just friendship, but Gavin was determined not to let that happen.

****

Thinking of the innocent, young Cody riding motorcycles made Madeline start thinking about Scott. She couldn't deal with those thoughts right now so she got up impatiently from her favorite, gray chair. After showering, she considered changing into her nightgown and robe, but on the off chance Gavin came by, she settled on a pair of sweatpants and a sweatshirt. Gavin seeing her in her night clothes was at the top of her list of things to not have happen.

Even that brief line of thinking led to a whole new set of images. If Gavin stopped by while she was in her gown...Madeline let the thought fall out of her consciousness, but she knew she would be thinking about him most of the night, whether he showed up or not.

She poured a glass of iced tea and settled into her chair once more. Madeline was wrapped in the pages of her book and enjoying the tea, thinking just maybe she would have the evening to herself. She froze when a familiar sound assailed her ears.

Chapter Five

Madeline choked on the iced tea she was drinking. Gavin must have decided he needed his money after all. Her coughing spell ended, but her heart raced and her palms were damp. Madeline knew the dampness had little to do with the glass she held. Confusion and desire washed over her like storm-tossed debris. Briefly, she considered ignoring the impatient summons. She was pretty sure Gavin wouldn't go away so she didn't have a choice other than to answer the door. Madeline knew it was him. There was no mistaking the sound of his motorcycle, and he was the only one who would show up at her house riding one. Reluctantly, she pulled herself from her chair and walked slowly to the door.

****

Waiting impatiently on the other side of the door, it was his desire for Madeline that occupied all of Gavin's thoughts. Never had he been less concerned about money. Even before he'd continued the ride with Cody and Dennis, he'd made up his mind to go to Madeline's house just as soon as they got back. When Gavin was about to knock again, Madeline opened the door.

"You told me earlier to knock if I needed something." Gavin stood there, his eyes glinting with dangerous intent. His leather jacket was nowhere in evidence, leaving his arms bare. The hot weather invited motorcyclists to abandon their heavy leathers.

In the back of her mind, Madeline knew it wasn't safe to ride like that, but safety was taking a distant back seat now as she looked at those powerful, muscled arms. *All those hard, rippling muscles.*

"Oh," Madeline walked back to her chair, "you must mean your check." She opened the drawer of the end table and pulled out an envelope.

She handed him the envelope without meeting his gaze. "Thank you again. I think a miracle happened in my yard."

Gavin willed her to meet his gaze, but so far no luck. He savored Madeline's fragrance which reminded him of the fresh air one feels on the beach. God, she was standing so close. He raised an arm to reach for her, but dropped it as quickly. His breathing shallow and rapid, he ran one hand over his mouth. "Just doing my job."

Gavin was certain Madeline wanted him as much as he wanted her, even if she wouldn't admit it. He saw the plea in her eyes and he understood that plea. He also knew that this was not the time to answer that plea. It took everything inside him to jump on his motorcycle and ride away from her house, pursued by the thought Madeline had the power to unhinge him completely.

****

Her face hot, her own breath coming in ragged gasps, Madeline took a few steps backwards, then turned and walked to the kitchen. She ran a glass of water from the tap, but instead of drinking it, she pressed the glass to her face. Her frustration and disappointment forced her to talk out loud.

"That's all this is to him? A job?"

"I don't think I can stand it if he doesn't kiss me soon. Yet, I don't want anything to do with him so why am I worrying about kissing him? I don't need to get involved with any man, let alone an irresponsible one. He certainly is irresponsible when he hauls a little kid around on his motorcycle." Madeline continued her audible self-debate.

"Gavin has a full-time job with the power company and he works part-time in his landscaping business. Plus in his favor, he did show up when he said he would to do my yard. As for Cody riding the bike, can I really see a problem? He was wearing a helmet, leather jacket and boots. Jeans. I know in this state children under age five can't ride on motorcycles. Hadn't Cody mentioned that he was seven?

"On the other hand, it was only once that Gavin showed up at my place on time. That's no reason to give him unlimited access to my life."

He's responsible.

Madeline didn't know where that voice had come from? Was her own heart turning on her?

The speed pushing Madeline to acceptance of Gavin made her quite dizzy and she shook her head to dispel further thoughts of him. No, the best thing she could do was keep him out of her life, as much as possible. Madeline could see that Gavin was too much of a good-time, party boy. She couldn't spare time for fun, not with a new job to adjust to. Also, that damn bike would always be a barrier between them since it would only serve as a direct and physical reminder of her brother. Maybe it was time to look for another landscaper.

Maybe Joe is right. It's time to stop living in the past.

That voice again!

She glanced at her watch and saw she had been lost in thought for nearly two hours. Damn. That man is turning my life upside down she said to herself.

****

Madeline wasn't the only one talking to herself. Across town, it was Gavin's turn to argue and debate with himself, silently and out loud. He had never wanted someone as much as he wanted Madeline, but it would be a union destined for failure. She seemed incapable of having fun and she apparently hated motorcycles. Gavin could tell from the look Madeline had given his bike. She would never accept his cycle, and without that acceptance, there could be no future for the two of them.

"Why in hell am I thinking about a future between us? That isn't going to happen so it doesn't matter what she thinks about motorcycles. Yet, I wonder why she hates bikes so much? What would she say if I asked her to go for a ride?" Gavin knew two things for sure. First, Madeline's anti-motorcycle attitude was totally unreasonable, but he wanted her in spite of that. Second, he wasn't going to ask her to go for a ride. Even as he had this thought, Gavin realized this was exactly what he would do the first chance he got.

****

Madeline still couldn't believe the mere sound of his voice caused the turmoil in her guts. To make matters worse, he appeared to recognize the effect it had on her. She saw the flash in his eyes.

Once again, Madeline was glad she had only signed a short-term lease on the house rather than buying. She knew she would love working with Joe, but if she couldn't control her feelings about Gavin, she would have to leave Heron's Cove.

No wonder I'm getting a headache. Lately when I have any time to think it's Gavin who occupies my thoughts. Tomorrow is my first official day at the hospital. I'll have some positive pegs to hang my thoughts on, ones that won't include him.

The phone rang and Madeline's heart pounded in her ears. She reached for the phone, hoping against hope it was Gavin. If it were, she would invite him back, or go to his house. Anything just to see him again. *So much for having other thoughts.*

"Hello?" Even to her own ears Madeline thought her voice sounded like it came from someone who had just sprinted up a few flights of stairs.

"Maddy, you sound out of breath. Where have you been? I know you haven't been out taking care of your yard."

"Very funny, Joe. I haven't been anywhere." Madeline fought hard to keep the keen disappointment from her voice. At the same time, she had the irrational feeling Joe knew exactly what had caused her breathlessness. She didn't want Joe to know how she felt about Gavin.

Madeline loved Joe, but she did wish he would stop trying to fix her up. Was that why he had recommended Gavin?

"Have you bothered to eat anything since you got home?" Joe wisely decided to let it go. "I know you often forget to eat. I just don't understand how anybody could do that."

As far as she knew, Joe had never forgotten a meal in his life. Then there were all the extras he consumed like banana splits, chips and dip and, of course, doughnuts.

Madeline laughed out loud when she heard this. "As a matter of fact, I was getting up to make a sandwich when you called."

"Don't forget, Maddy. As the new person, it's your responsibility to bring doughnuts to work tomorrow."

"Joe, for the sake of your health and mine, I've a good mind to bring a vegetable tray instead."

"Please say you won't do that."

"No, Joe, I won't. I'll bring the doughnuts."

Madeline smiled as she hung up the phone. She knew the call was another way Joe was giving her his support. She was sure he felt responsible for bringing her to Heron's Cove and was worried she would blame him if things didn't work out.

Madeline wished she could be more like Joe. He was a total extrovert and he didn't let much of anything bother him. Madeline wasn't nearly as outgoing as Joe, and tended to let things get under her skin. Things that shouldn't bother her. Oh well, it was something she could work on in the coming months.

After she ate her sandwich, Madeline lay down on the bed. Her plan was to rest for a while and then do some work on her computer. She had no intention of going to sleep for the night. Her planned quick nap blended into a much longer sleep, but she didn't enjoy an easy sleep. She tossed around, indefinable images darting in and out of her nighttime vulnerability. One of the images eventually took shape and spoke to her. This wasn't the first time.

****

"Come on, Chicken, get up. It's time to go." Her brother stood at the foot of the bed, fully dressed and holding something under his left arm. Chicken had been a term of endearment Scott used for his sister. The name had nothing to do with bravery or lack of it, but stemmed from the fact Madeline, at one time, had a pet chicken that followed her everywhere.

She started to answer him, to tell him it was much too early to go anywhere, but the words stuck in her throat. She bolted awake, her body awash in cold sweat. Scott was no longer in the room.

Her logical side said that she had just experienced a dream of some sort, but her emotional side wasn't listening. Her eyes swept the room, searching for any

40

piece of concrete evidence that Scott had been in the room minutes before. Of course, she found nothing and her eyes stopped on the bedside clock, which reflected the red numbers showing it was just after four a.m.

Madeline knew she wouldn't be able to fall back asleep in the bedroom after seeing Scott so she picked up a pillow and blanket and headed for the couch.

She recalled the conversation she'd had with Joe after the last nightmare. It had been on one of her visits to Heron's Cove.

"Maddy, you look awful," Joe had said when she stumbled out from the guest bedroom. "It was that same nightmare again, wasn't it?" He was well aware of Madeline's recurring dreams, which usually left her near hysteria.

"Yes...uh, no...I mean...I'm not sure exactly. Scott was here this morning, standing at the foot of my bed. He looked so real. I thought I could touch him. H...he called me Chicken. He told me to get up, but when I did, he was gone." Madeline now seemed close to tears. Joe took her in his arms and held her gently.

When she seemed a little calmer, Joe had spoken again.

"Have you thought of talking to someone, Maddy?"

Seconds ticked by while Madeline considered her response.

"I am pretty sure, Joe, that I shared with you what happened when I saw a therapist in Seattle. I didn't feel like it did any good." Madeline wiggled impatiently and broke from Joe's embrace.

"Maybe it didn't do any good because you didn't let it," Joe had said, bracing himself for an argument. "If I remember correctly, you only saw him a couple of times."

"How could he possibly have helped me, Joe?" Madeline asked. "All he wanted to talk about was the accident."

"That actually makes sense, Madeline. After all, Scott's accident was the reason you were seeing a therapist in the first place. What did you think he'd talk about? Fishing? Football? The ballet?"

"I didn't want to talk about the accident then and I

don't want to talk about it now. As a matter of fact, I'd be ecstatic if I didn't ever have to think about it again. Talking about it won't bring Scott back."

Joe had been quiet for a while, his eyes clouded with sadness. "You're right, Maddy, but maybe if you talked to someone, the nightmares would stop."

Now, stretching out on the couch, Madeline thought it might be a good sign that the nightmares weren't as frequent. "Scott, it doesn't mean I'm forgetting about you. I'll never do that." Madeline wondered if Joe had been right when he suggested she talk with someone again.

****

Monday morning Madeline had a visit from her next-door neighbor. Emma Perry was seventy-two, but her age didn't slow her down at all. Madeline delighted in listening to her soft British accent. *Mom will love meeting her when she returns from her visit to England.* Madeline's mother was visiting friends and was due home in a couple of weeks.

"Good morning, Mrs. Perry." Madeline extended her hand to the little woman standing at her door.

"It is a lovely morning, isn't it, dear?"

"Would you like to come in?" Madeline asked.

"Just for a minute, dear. I know you're on your way to work." Emma Perry came in and perched on the edge of Madeline's couch. "I may have occasion to ask for your help with my cat, Tobias. He climbs the tree in my backyard and won't come down."

"Mrs. Perry," Madeline said, "he'll come down when he gets hungry."

"Oh no, not Tobias. I've asked other neighbors for help before, and once I even called the fire department. But since you're a veterinarian, I thought you'd have better success."

"Well, if Tobias gets stuck, I'll be glad to help." Privately she thought what goes up must come down. Or get extremely hungry.

Madeline offered coffee, which her visitor declined.

At last Mrs. Perry got around to addressing the reason for her visit, although she would never have admitted it was the main reason.

"My dear," she began. "I noticed a motorcycle parked in your driveway on several occasions. And that guy..." her neighbor leaned forward just a bit, "...he's hot."

Madeline choked on her sip of coffee, nearly spraying it through her nose. "Mrs. Perry!"

Now it was Emma Perry's turn to laugh. When her merriment subsided, she said, "I may be old, but I'm not dead yet. When I get too old to appreciate a stud like that, I'll know it's time for me to go into the home."

"Forgive me. I'm not usually so bold," she continued, "but surely you must have noticed him. I mean as young and beautiful as you are."

"That was the landscaper." Madeline swallowed and wiped away the tears caused by her coughing spell. "Actually he was only here three times. The first time he came to see the yard, then he was here to do the work and then he came back because he had forgotten his money. So, yes, I noticed him." Oh, how Madeline had noticed Gavin. Although she wasn't about to share with Emma Perry, Madeline had a keen sensation her neighbor already knew it.

"Well, I, for one, certainly hope he comes by again, especially on that bike." Mrs. Perry's smile reminded Madeline of a young girl in love for the first time. "Do you suppose he would take me for a ride?

"I'm sure he would, Mrs. Perry. I'll ask him when he comes to do the yard next time." Madeline knew how much Mrs. Perry would love a ride since the older woman had once shared her own childhood stories about riding as a girl in England.

"Good. One more thing, dear. You and I are going to be friends, so you must call me Emma."

"All right, I will." Madeline walked her guest to the door, then locked up and headed for the garage.

First Joe, now Emma. Was everyone in Heron's Cove on Gavin's side? *Am I the only person who wants nothing to do with him?* When Mom comes to visit I absolutely have to keep her and Gavin apart. She knew her mother and Gavin would form a mutual admiration society, and Madeline didn't want to face the two against one force those two would put up against her.

Patty Hardin

44

Chapter Six

When Madeline got up at seven the next morning she was grateful dreams hadn't disturbed her sleep. Not only that, the weather was spectacular. Blue sky. Sunshine. Perfection. She definitely felt refreshed and ready to face her first day at the hospital. About halfway to work, however, the weather took a back seat when a familiar whup, whup, whup signaled a flat tire.

"Oh shit." Madeline started to apologize for her language. "Madeline Spencer, you are losing it. There's nobody in the car to hear the apology."

She was capable of changing the tire, but she didn't want to deal with it, especially not on her first day of work. It would mean getting dirty and greasy so she would have to go back home, shower and change clothes, all of which would make her late to work. Being late to work was one thing Madeline had a difficult time dealing with. At least she had a good spot to pull over. Madeline was thankful she had put a full-size spare in the trunk to replace the little doughnut tire. Before she got out of the car, she called the hospital to say she might be late and would be in as soon as she changed the tire.

****

Gavin was on his way to work when he spotted Madeline's car pulled over on the opposite side of the road. At first glance, he noticed she seemed to be having problems with the tire changing process. He knew the polite thing to do would be crossing to that side of the road and offering help, even though he knew such an offer might very well be rejected. Gavin turned around and pulled up behind Madeline's car, prepared to offer assistance.

Madeline had a wrench in her hand and was attempting to loosen the first lug nut when Gavin pulled up behind her car. "Morning. Need some help?"

"No, thank you, I've got it handled." Madeline stood up, brushing a strand of hair from her eyes, leaving a smudge of grease on her forehead.

"Hmm. I can see that." Gavin couldn't take his eyes from Madeline's face. Even the grease mark on her forehead was attractive. "Here, let me." He reached for the wrench but all he wanted to do was take Madeline in his arms. With luck maybe the tire would fix itself. Gavin shook these thoughts from his head and went to work.

When he saw the full sized tire, Gavin couldn't help but think, *here is a woman who must know something about cars.*

****

Madeline relinquished the wrench with a small protest, standing silently while Gavin went to work on the tire. She wasn't sure, but it sounded like he was swearing, which actually got a little bit of a smile out of her. However, she was sure Gavin looked every bit as gorgeous now as he did the first time she saw him. *I still wonder what it would feel like to be kissed by this man with that glorious mustache.* Madeline's mind was definitely not on her flat tire.

"Who tightened these lug nuts anyway?" he asked.

"A mechanic in Seattle," Madeline said stiffly. "I had the tires rotated just before I moved down here."

"No wonder you were having trouble getting these off. He must have been a sadistic son of a ..." Gavin stopped himself. "Sorry."

At six feet four inches tall, Gavin was nearly a foot taller than Madeline's five feet six inches and obviously much stronger. The fact he was having trouble removing the lug nuts made Madeline feel less helpless and foolish for depending on a man to help her.

With the tire finally changed, they worked together to put the flat and the tools away. Madeline was once again ready to head for work. She started to open the driver's door, then remembered she hadn't thanked Gavin for his assistance. Because of his efforts, she wouldn't be any more than five minutes late to work, if that much. Before she could say anything, Gavin spoke to her.

"Madeline." That one word stopped her as surely as if Gavin had physically restrained her. "Go for a ride with me; I mean us, tomorrow afternoon. Me, Cody, his dad."

Before Madeline's throat could close around the one word reply, it slipped out.

"Okay."

Their gazes locked and held.

"What time do you get off work?" Gavin asked. She noticed he was trying very hard not to smile.

"Five o'clock," Madeline said, in a voice she barely recognized as her own.

"I'll pick you up at six. Don't worry about gear. Between me and Dennis, we have duplicates of nearly everything."

Gavin was on his bike and moving away while Madeline still stood by her car. Finally she got in, her eyes on the rear-view mirror watching Gavin disappear. As she sat in the car trying to reign in her racing heart, she noticed the grease mark on her forehead. *Oh my gosh, was that there the entire time?* The red coloring on her cheeks from embarrassment competed with the red on her forehead from her efforts to wipe away the mark.

Kelly, the receptionist and assistant, looked up when the front door opened.

"Good morning, Dr. Spencer," she said.

"Good morning, Kelly. Please, call me Madeline. Dr. Spencer makes me feel so old." She had met Kelly earlier when she first toured the hospital with Joe.

"Okay, you got it." Kelly had been with Joe since he opened the hospital, and Joe was trying to convince her to go for her degree in veterinary medicine. Madeline hoped there might be something going on between Joe and Kelly.

Joe came out of his office just then. "So, are you looking forward to your first day at the hospital?" he asked.

"I sure am." A big smile suffused Madeline's features. "When I helped Dennis with his parrot, I was reminded why I chose this field in the first place. I was upset at first because I thought Gavin and Dennis were being irresponsible about the bird. In a way I guess they were, but Gavin felt so bad about letting the bird out, I couldn't be mad any more. Rescuing the parrot was the important thing and we did that. I am definitely ready to jump in with both feet."

"I don't have any appointments for this morning, so I'll be on hand to help out in case things get too hectic," Joe said.

"The busier I am, the better it will be," Madeline replied.

"One thing's for sure. A lot of people already know you're in town, even though the article hasn't come out yet. They'll come by the hospital just to get a look at the new doc. After all, you are from the big city."

"I hope they'll find out I really will be able to help them with their animals. I don't want to be just a curiosity item," Madeline said.

"If I'm not mistaken," Joe leaned against the wall, arms crossed and smiling, "Dennis is already spreading the word about your abilities. Gavin probably is, too."

"I guess we'll see, won't we?" Madeline asked. "What does our schedule look like?" She shrugged into her lab coat.

Kelly consulted the day's schedule. "Busy, but just the usual shots and exams. Nothing major. I think a lot of the people just want to meet you, Madeline."

"You mean get a look at me."

"That, too," Kelly said, her laugh like a touch of spring on a gloomy day.

Madeline laughed, too, and prepared to meet her first patient, a dog coming in for a rabies shot.

Just as Kelly had said, the morning was busier than even Madeline had thought it would be. When they finally reached a lull just before noon, Madeline decided the animals in Heron's Cove had to be among the healthiest in the world.

Not being sure how busy the morning would be, Madeline had brought her lunch. After the last morning patient, she and Kelly sat in the break room to eat and unwind.

"You know, it's kind of sad," Kelly said, taking a sip of her soda.

"What is?" Madeline asked between bites.

"The people in this town spend so much on taking care of their animals. I mean, it's good they care about their pets, and of course, it's good for us..." Kelly grinned, "but sometimes, I think, a few of them neglect themselves in order to have money for their animals."

Madeline had had the same thought when she was taking care of her four-legged patients.

"I suppose you're right, Kelly, but just remember this. It's their choice and caring for their pets makes these people feel good."

When Kelly got up to answer the phone, Madeline was left with her thoughts about the next day and the ride she had agreed to take with Gavin. *What would he say if he knew I used to have all my own riding gear and my own motorcycle?*

Joe got back to the hospital just before five o'clock, showing little sign of his afternoon's hard work. He washed up, took his lab coat off the hook and sat down for a catch up session with Madeline.

"We're still on for dinner tonight, right?" Joe asked after Madeline had brought him current with the afternoon's happenings at the hospital. "Seven o'clock?"

"You bet," Madeline answered. "Do you want me to bring anything?"

"No. I have it all under control."

"What are you serving anyway?"

"Sorry, Maddy. I can't tell you, but you'll like it. I promise," Joe said.

Madeline got up to walk the two boarder dogs, but Kelly already had them out and ready for their walk. "Thanks, Kelly. See you in the morning." Madeline stopped long enough to pet the dogs on her way out.

****

The second she stepped through Joe's door that night Madeline knew he had chosen something from one of his garlic cookbooks. The house smelled like a gourmet restaurant.

"You won't believe what I did today," Madeline said as she helped Joe clean up after their dinner of garlic shrimp, pasta, salad and garlic bread.

"Well, you said you had a flat tire on the way to work." Joe busied himself putting detergent in the cups inside the dishwasher. "But you've changed tires before so that's no big deal."

"The flat tire is only a small part of the story, and by the way, I didn't change it myself."

"Who did?"

"Gavin Marshall." Once again, Madeline had cause to wonder as Joe smiled as if he was trying to set her up with Gavin.

"There's a story here and I'm ready to hear it."

"Don't get your hopes up, Joe. There's not much to tell. I was struggling to loosen the first lug nut when he pulled up behind me and asked if I needed help. Of course I said no, but it was obvious to him I couldn't get the nut loose. He had a hard time with it, too, I might add, which definitely made me feel a little better about not being able to do it myself."

"There's more to your story, isn't there?" Joe poured glasses of white wine for himself and Madeline. "Maddy?"

"As a matter of fact, yes."

They took their glasses and went outside to sit on lounge chairs on Joe's back deck.

"Well?" Joe asked, once they were seated.

"When the tire was changed and everything put away, Gavin asked me to go for a ride with him and Dennis on Tuesday." She stopped to take a deep breath and looked around the backyard trying to stall.

"Madeline, if you don't finish your story, I'll...well...I don't know what I'll do. Just tell me, okay?" Joe had forgotten his wine. "What did you say?"

"The invitation was so sudden, so unexpected. Before I could stop myself, I said okay."

"Good for you, Madeline. I went for a ride with Gavin once. I kept telling him I didn't want to go, but he can be pretty persuasive. It was cool. I was a little scared, but bikes weren't a part of my life like they were of yours and Scott's."

This was indeed true. The Spencers had tried to interest Joe in riding motorcycles, but it just hadn't been his forte.

"I'm sure Gavin knows several people, mostly women, who would be more than willing to ride with him."

"No doubt he does," Joe said, "but he asked you, not one of those other people."

"Joe, you're not trying to fix us up, are you?"

"Of course not, Maddy."

Madeline didn't think Joe's answer rang true. She noticed he didn't look at her when he said it, but she let the matter drop.

"I still may change my mind, Joe."

"Madeline Spencer, you will do no such thing. You *will* go on that ride tomorrow and you *will* enjoy it."

"I don't know why I should go or enjoy it. I haven't changed my mind. I still think motorcycles are far too dangerous for anybody to ride let alone a little kid like Cody."

"This is all about Scott, isn't it?" Joe asked. "Maddy, what happened with Scott is in the past. You need to talk it out with somebody and then get on with your life."

Madeline could feel the color flaming to her cheeks.

"Go ahead, Maddy. Be angry with me. Hit me, if you need to, but you know I'm right. It's been twelve years since Scott's accident. You need to start living your life in the present."

"Are you telling me to forget about my brother, to act like he never existed? Well, I can't. I won't do that, Joe."

"Of course, I'm not asking you to forget Scott. He was my friend, as well as your brother." Joe reached out to touch Madeline's arm. "I thought you wanted a fresh start, Maddy. That's one of the reasons I offered you the partnership. However, if you're not willing to meet me at least part way on this, maybe you aren't ready for that new start after all. Maybe I made a mistake by asking you to move down here."

"You're giving up on me; is that it?"

"Don't be ridiculous, Madeline. If that was the case, I would never have told you about the partnership."

Madeline was silent, unsure what to think or feel at this point. When she looked up at him, the flaming red had all but left her face.

"Joe, just by saying I'd go on the ride I managed to

loose all the demons I've tried so hard to keep hidden. Cody reminds me so much of Scott; he even looks like Scott did at that age. He's just as eager as Scott was about riding." Madeline's breathing was rapid, but she refused to cry even though her heart felt like it was breaking all over again.

Joe put his arms around her and held her close. "You're the only person who can stop your slide toward that dark place."

When Madeline settled into a normal pattern of breathing, Joe spoke, his voice soothing like some ancient, mystical balm.

"Maddy, whether you know it or not, you made a huge step just now by talking about Scott. By telling Gavin you'd go on that ride, you took an even bigger step. Take the ride, enjoy yourself. You deserve to."

When Madeline got home, the delectable dinner she had enjoyed with Joe was all but forgotten as she struggled to stabilize her flailing emotions. Joe was right about so many things. Madeline wondered if he was right when he said she deserved to enjoy herself. His advice was usually sound, given after a lot of thought and without judgment.

Madeline thought about something else Joe had said during their talk. Scott had been his friend. That was so true it made Madeline smile now. In a way it was like she had two brothers. Joe had been a part of the Spencer family since he and Madeline became friends in the seventh grade. Likewise, Madeline and Scott had been members of the Bingham family.

With all of that, though, Joe was wrong about Scott. Even though Joe knew everything about the accident, Madeline knew she'd never convince him, or anyone else, that she was responsible for what had happened to her brother. The therapist she saw in Seattle tried to tell her it was survivor's guilt she was experiencing, but Madeline knew he was wrong. Scott had so much to offer. He should still be here.

She didn't hesitate long before picking up the phone and punching in Gavin's number.

Chapter Seven

Madeline held her breath and couldn't even release it when Gavin answered in a voice she not only recognized, but also was beginning to crave. To be honest, she craved most things about this man. She hung up without uttering a word.

Preparing for bed, Madeline told herself she would only cancel the ride if she had a good solid reason for doing so. As hard as she tried, she couldn't find even a weak reason.

It took Madeline what seemed like hours to fall asleep only to have it disturbed by those faceless, nameless dreams one doesn't recall clearly the next morning. One image, however, had been so clear it seemed real. It was of Gavin astride his motorcycle in her driveway, smiling and saying, "Come on, Babe. Let's ride."

Tuesday morning found Madeline in full recall of what would be taking place after work. She hated to admit it, but she was looking forward to it.

No flat tire slowed her progress this morning and she arrived at the hospital to find another full schedule of patients. Joe would be spending at least the morning hours helping Madeline. It promised to be a long day for the two doctors and guaranteed no homemade dinners for either one of them.

Madeline's second patient that morning was a yellow-naped Amazon parrot. Its treatment would call on her diplomatic skills as well as her medical ones. The bird, brought in by a little boy and his mother, was in to have its flight feathers trimmed and its toenails cut, but Madeline soon saw an opportunity to offer dietary advice.

The child was eating a chocolate bar and the bird was doing its best to snag a piece. Of course, the little boy obliged.

When it was his bird's turn in one of the exam rooms, Madeline invited the little boy to come along.

"I noticed you sharing your candy bar with your bird," Madeline said, clipping the toenails as Kelly held the bird wrapped in a towel.

"Uh, huh. He likes it," the little boy said, looking up at Madeline.

"Well, sharing your food or your toys can be a good thing," Madeline released the bird to the child's mother, "but there are some things you shouldn't share."

"Like what?" the boy asked.

"Well, you shouldn't share chocolate with your bird."

"Why?" The little boy looked at Madeline like she was just another grown-up giving orders.

"Chocolate can make your bird very sick."

"I eat it and it doesn't make me sick." The child thrust his chin out with a defiant look in his eyes.

"I believe you," Madeline said, "but that's because your tummy is very different from your bird's tummy."

The little boy said nothing as the three of them walked out of the exam room; the bird quietly grumbling over what he perceived as bad treatment.

"I have a list of forbidden foods and plants for birds I can send home with you," Madeline said to the mother.

"I'd really appreciate it," she said, ready to pay her bill. "Thank you, Dr. Spencer."

They were too busy for most of the day to have any long conversations, but Joe asked her a couple of times if she had changed her mind about riding with Gavin that afternoon. She assured him she was still going, but she could tell he didn't really believe her, especially since she told him about calling Gavin.

"But, Joe, I hung up when he answered. I didn't say a word."

Even though Joe dropped the subject, Madeline caught his raised eyebrow directed at her a few times the rest of the day.

When they finally locked the doors at almost five-thirty that night, Madeline and Joe looked at each other, hungry and exhausted.

"I don't know about you, Maddy, but that doughnut I

had earlier might as well have been nothing. I'm starving."

"Joe, you know doughnuts aren't really good for you, but that orange I had didn't fill me up, either. Now the question is, what are you doing about dinner? I'm too nervous to eat much so I'll wait until after the ride."

"I suppose it's takeout for me," Joe said.

Madeline set about dressing for the ride when she got home. Gavin had said he would bring the gear she needed so she put on jeans, a long-sleeved shirt and boots that covered her ankles. Her hair was still held back in its single braid so she left it that way. Glancing at the clock on her nightstand, Madeline saw she had only ten minutes before Gavin arrived. Idly, she wondered if Emma Perry was watching from her front porch and pictured herself riding away with the man she called "hot". Too bad Madeline couldn't disagree.

****

At six o'clock the low thunder of motorcycle engines told Madeline the time was at hand. Recognizing the fact she no longer *wanted* to back out, she answered the door when Gavin knocked.

He looked pleased, and genuinely surprised, to see Madeline dressed and ready to go.

"You're really going," he said, his broad smile giving his approval to her clothing.

When Madeline stepped outside she saw Cody and his dad waiting on their bike. She turned back to lock the door, listening to Gavin's advice as she did so.

"Madeline, if you want to end the ride at any time, for any reason, just tap my left leg three times. I'll take you home immediately. No questions asked."

"Understood," Madeline said, looking up at Gavin.

They walked over to the bikes and Gavin started introducing Madeline to Cody's dad before he recalled Mako's escape. "That's right. You two have already met."

Madeline and Dennis shook hands. "How's Mako doing?"

"Just fine, none the worse for his little escapade." Denny brought out a leather jacket, helmet and gloves for her to wear.

"This is my sister's gear," Dennis said. "She's a little bigger than you are, but the jacket and gloves should still be a pretty good fit."

Madeline found out this was indeed true. She put the helmet on and waited for Gavin to restart the engine before she got on the motorcycle behind him.

They had decided to ride to the lighthouse on the bluff overlooking the ocean, north of Heron's Cove. There they could walk around for a little while before riding back. Madeline recognized they were doing this mostly for her benefit and she appreciated their consideration.

Not long into the ride, Madeline stopped trembling. She wasn't sure if it was fear or excitement that caused her shaking; she suspected it was a combination of both.

When they had dismounted, Madeline looked up at Gavin, beaming.

"You've ridden before."

"Some," Madeline replied, still smiling. "I knew what to wear and that you had to get on the bike first. Oh, and leaning with you in the turns."

"More than that," Gavin said.

Madeline was surprised to discover she didn't mind telling Gavin about her riding history.

"I started riding when I was five. When I was ten, I started racing and kept that up until I was fifteen."

"Why did you stop?" Gavin asked.

"I decided school was more important and I couldn't do justice to both racing and studies. I kept on riding, but just for fun."

At a break in the adults' conversation, Cody piped up.

"Dad, I'm hungry."

"Cody," his father said in mock exasperation, "you're always hungry. But yes, to put your mind at ease, we will stop for something to eat.

"Would you and Madeline like to join us?" Dennis asked.

"Sure," Gavin said.

"Count me in," Madeline said.

They got back on their bikes and headed for the little hamburger shop at the edge of town.

Madeline enjoyed an easy conversation with the

three guys. They talked about her adjustment to Heron's Cove, motorcycles and the pros and cons of their respective jobs. Madeline decided to share Emma Perry's opinions of motorcycle riders.

"My neighbor noticed your bike in my driveway." Madeline looked at Gavin. "She's quite impressed with you and wondered if you'd take her for a ride sometime." Madeline wasn't about to share Emma Perry's opinion that Gavin was hot, although she had to smile to herself as she thought about it.

"I've got a job in your neighborhood tomorrow," Gavin said, looking at Madeline. "Maybe I'll stop by and talk to her."

"That would make her day." And mine, Madeline thought.

Madeline was sorry to see the evening end.

They pulled up in her driveway a little after nine o'clock. She got off the bike to return the gear and thank Cody and Dennis for the loan.

"My sister moved to California," Dennis told her. "Keep it as long as you want."

"Thank you," Madeline said. "And thanks for including me on the ride tonight. I had fun."

It surprised her when Gavin also dismounted and walked with her to the front door.

"Thank you for tonight," Madeline said, slipping the key in the lock.

"I hope you enjoyed the ride, at least somewhat," Gavin said.

"I did," Madeline said, "although I called last night to cancel."

"I thought that might have been you. What changed your mind?"

"I'm not sure." Madeline wasn't about to admit it was because she wanted to see Gavin again.

She was aware of the two people waiting on the second bike in the driveway, yet was reluctant to let go of the tenuous connection between her and Gavin.

"Uh," Gavin began, and then stopped as if unsure of himself. "Look, I'd like to see you again." The words came out in a rush.

"I'd like to see you again, too." Madeline was shocked to realize she meant the words as she smiled up at Gavin. "Call me when you get home."

"Okay. I will." He leaned down and kissed her on the cheek. Madeline watched him turn and hurry down to his bike while she seemed frozen in the moment. Her fingers trembled as they touched her cheek and a small sigh rushed past them.

****

Madeline walked inside, her step lighter than it had been in awhile. With their busy schedules, she knew the opportunities for them to go riding, or anyplace else, were limited. However, she was looking forward to seeing him again. It seemed ages ago that she had been so determined to keep Gavin out of her life.

The red light blinking on the answering machine told Madeline she had a message.

"Maddy, call me." Joe was expecting a full report on the ride. Madeline had to chuckle as she tried to think about what to tell him while dialing the phone. He picked up the phone before the first ring had faded.

"So, did you have a good time?" he asked.

"Yes, I did, and that is all I have time to share tonight. I just wanted you to know I got your message and I am home just fine. I have to hang up now as I'm waiting for a call. I'll tell you all about it tomorrow. Good night, Joe." She hung up on his voice still clamoring for details of her evening.

Too keyed up to concentrate on reading, Madeline kicked off her boots and sat down in her old, gray chair. She flipped on the TV and waited for Gavin to call.

He did, about twenty minutes after leaving Madeline's house.

"Hello?" She was irritated to hear herself sounding like a breathless teenager.

"Hi, Madeline." Gavin sounded much more relaxed now that they had time and privacy to talk.

They chatted at some length about the ride they had just taken and life in general, before the conversation rolled around to their individual plans for the coming weekend.

"It's been a hectic first week," Madeline said. "I'm just looking forward to sleeping in and then going grocery shopping. After that I'll probably do something exciting like take a nap. Sounds boring, doesn't it?" The words had been bad enough in her head but to actually say them out loud sounded incredibly boring.

"I'm taking a rare Saturday off," Gavin said. "If the weather holds, I'm going for a long ride. Too much time has passed since I've done that."

"That sounds good," Madeline said. "I hope the weather cooperates for you." At the same time she wondered where and if she might fit into Gavin's plan.

A brief pause followed before he asked, "Will you come with me?"

"Sure," Madeline answered.

"How about we go to Portland? We could wander around there awhile, have dinner some place and ride home. Do you have any objection to getting up early on your day off?" Gavin asked.

"That depends," Madeline said, hoping her voice conveyed a sense of lightness, not whining. "What do you consider early?"

"Around eight?" Gavin said.

Springing through quick mental calculations, Madeline figured she would have to get up no later than six-thirty. "Here's a thought," she said. "Come over earlier, say seven o'clock, and I'll have breakfast ready."

"Now there's a combination I can't pass up," Gavin said. "A beautiful woman who's cooking breakfast for me."

On this light note Gavin and Madeline said their good-byes.

****

Joe was ready for her Friday morning. Luckily, their first patient wouldn't be in until eleven because he wanted to hear all about the ride. Madeline obliged, almost feeling like a giddy teenager.

"Maybe you were right, Joe," she said, "when you told me I needed to move on."

"Of course, I was right."

"But wait until you hear part two of my tale."

"I'm not willing to wait much longer," Joe settled

himself down into his chair. "Talk to me."

"Well...Gavin asked me to ride with him to Portland tomorrow," Madeline said, enjoying the stunned look passing over her friend's face.

After a long pause, Joe leaned forward in his chair, "And?"

"And...I said yes."

"Madeline Spencer, you're on a roll now. You go for it girl."

"Joe," Madeline said, her tone growing serious, "riding around Heron's Cove is one thing. That was fun; I will admit I enjoyed it. But going to Portland means traffic and lots of it. I'll be out there, vulnerable, at the mercy of all those crazy drivers. Last night was my first ride in more than thirteen years. Now I'll be on a motorcycle in big city traffic? I'm scared, Joe."

"Of course you are, Maddy," Joe said, covering her hands with his own. "Tell me something. Do you trust Gavin?"

"Yes, I do," Madeline answered. "I felt safe riding with him last night and I never thought I'd feel like that again."

"Then go on the ride and have fun. Gavin won't let anything happen to you."

Before Madeline got up to see her patient, she invited Joe to her house for dinner Sunday night.

Later that afternoon, Madeline hadn't been home five minutes when she answered the door to find Emma Perry standing there, looking desperate.

"You've got to help me," she said.

"What's wrong, Emma?" Madeline asked.

"Tobias—my cat. He's stuck up in a tree again. You have to help me get him down." Emma Perry had already started down the steps, obviously certain Madeline would immediately follow her.

Madeline's first inclination was to tell Emma that if Tobias got up in the tree then he could certainly get himself down. Instead she told her neighbor to wait while she put on her shoes.

"Do you have a ladder, Emma?" Madeline asked.

"Of course I do," the old lady answered, turning

around to look at Madeline.

Gavin drove up just as Madeline started toward Emma's house. He pulled up to the curb and got out of his truck.

"Hi, Madeline," he said, walking over to where the two women now stood.

She returned his greeting and then introduced him to Emma.

"I'm going over to get her cat out of the tree," Madeline told him.

"Let me give you a hand," Gavin said.

Emma stood by nervously twisting a tissue in her hands, watching Gavin climb the ladder to rescue the errant Tobias.

"Here you go," Gavin said five minutes later as he handed the cat to his owner.

"Thank you," Emma said, looking Gavin over. "I knew from the first time I saw you that you were an angel." There was a definite gleam in her eye. "Maybe you'd consider taking me for a ride sometime."

Chapter Eight

Madeline took a long, leisurely shower when she got home Friday night. She got into her pajamas and climbed into bed, intending to read for a few minutes. She didn't get the chance to open the covers of her book because as soon as her body touched the mattress and her head settled on the pillow, Madeline was sound asleep. Her book lay untouched on the nightstand, the pages fluttering lightly in the breeze from the open window.

She awoke the next morning at six, feeling uneasy even though her sleep had been restful. Madeline couldn't recall any dreams from the previous night, so her nervousness didn't make sense to her right away. Then she realized it was Saturday, and she remembered telling Gavin she would ride to Portland with him. The butterflies in her stomach were doing the two-step, but Madeline gave no thought this morning to calling Gavin and cancelling. Instead, she showered, dressed and gathered ingredients in the kitchen for breakfast. She smiled as she caught herself humming a show tune.

Just before seven o'clock, she heard Gavin pull up in the driveway and went to open the door. Her heart hammered in her chest, though whether from excitement over seeing Gavin or fear of the upcoming ride she couldn't have said.

"Good morning, Ms. Spencer," Gavin smiled as he stepped inside.

"Good morning, Mr. Marshall." Madeline returned his formal greeting with one of her own. They both broke out in a fit of giggling.

"My, but we are formal. Let's try calling each other by our first names."

"Yes, ma'am." After a brief pause Gavin added, "Dr. Spencer."

The laughter exploded again as Madeline showed him into the kitchen.

"I hope you're hungry, because breakfast is ready."

They sat down to a scrumptious offering of scrambled eggs, sausage, toast and orange juice. Madeline had also brewed a fresh pot of coffee.

"Let me help with the dishes," Gavin said when they had finished breakfast.

"Thanks, but that isn't necessary," Madeline told him. "It'll just take me a few minutes." She took the dishes to the sink, rinsed them off and put them in the dishwasher.

"Just as the other day, Madeline, if you want to stop the ride at any time let me know. I don't want you to ride if you're frightened or uncomfortable."

"I appreciate that, I really do. But I'm not expecting to be scared. Okay, maybe a little tense at first, but not enough to cancel the ride."

By eight o'clock, they were on the bike headed to Portland. The weather was beautiful, which meant the traffic was heavy, at least in Madeline's opinion. When they first merged onto the freeway, Madeline drew a deep breath and tightened her grip on Gavin's waist. *I shouldn't have done this. I'm not ready to ride. Maybe I never will be.* She pried her left hand from Gavin's waist, prepared to tap his leg. Something made her hesitate and soon her hand was locked once more on Gavin's waist. Before long, though, she loosened that grip and sat up straighter. More than halfway to their first stop Madeline leaned back, her hands resting lightly on Gavin's waist.

When they stopped for fuel and Madeline got off the bike, her legs shook so hard she wondered if they would hold her.

"Madeline, are you okay?" Gavin put his arm around her shoulders.

She nodded. "It was a little scarier than I thought it would be, at least at first. When we went on the freeway I actually raised my hand to tap your leg."

"You wanted to go home?" Gavin asked.

Madeline nodded again. "I thought I did." She looked up at Gavin, beaming. "Then I found myself relaxing and actually let go of my death grip on your waist and really started enjoying the ride. I'm starting to realize how much I've missed it." She stretched long and hard. "Of course, I am also finding old riding muscles that haven't been used in awhile."

"I knew on Tuesday that you'd ridden before. It takes years to be as fluid as you feel back there. I take it you want to continue."

"You take it right," Madeline said. "On to Portland."

Blue sky and sunshine combined to make their day in Portland beautiful. The weather held for them as they meandered through a street fair, stopping at one point to enjoy an impromptu jazz concert. Any possibility of rain was like a distant bad memory.

"Tell me about yourself, Madeline Spencer," Gavin said, taking her hand as they continued their walk.

"What do you want to know?" Madeline countered.

"I know you moved to Heron's Cove from Seattle," Gavin began. "Is that where you're from?"

"I was born and raised there. I never lived any place else except for the years at veterinary school in Pullman. I've traveled a lot, though. Let's see. Sturgis once, when I was fifteen. Hawaii. And I spent a year in England as an exchange student when I was a junior in high school."

"What did you think about Sturgis?"

"It was pretty overwhelming for a young girl, but all the same it was awesome."

"Did Scott go?" Gavin asked.

"He did." Madeline chuckled at the long ago memory.

"How was it for him?" Gavin asked, wondering what made her laugh.

"He was only twelve, so I think he was embarrassed by some of the stuff he saw, even though Mom and Dad did a good job of telling him about it ahead of time. I know his face was pretty red the whole time we were there and it wasn't all from the sun. Poor kid. Have you been?"

"Twice, and I want to go again. Do you miss Seattle?"

"I miss the things Seattle can offer, like concerts, the theatre and basketball games. But I don't miss them enough to move back."

"Do you have family there?" Gavin asked.

"My mother still lives there," Madeline said. "She's visiting friends in England at the moment."

They walked in an easy silence for a little while before either one said anything else.

"Your mother probably wouldn't be too happy to know you're charging around the country with a motorcycle outlaw." Gavin said.

"Are you kidding? If she were here right now, she'd push me aside and take my place."

"You're not serious."

"Oh yes, I am. My mom and dad were riding bikes long before they met each other. Sometimes I think I must have been born on one."

"Your mother is somebody I'd definitely like to meet."

"You'll get your chance soon enough," Madeline said. "She called on Thursday and will be back from England a week from Saturday. I know she'll be down here for a visit soon after."

"Any chance she'll ride down?"

"There's a very good chance of that," Madeline said, "unless the weather turns completely rotten. I used to refuse to ride in the rain, but Mom is such a diehard rider rain usually doesn't stop her."

Madeline paused for a moment as she thought more introspectively. "I know my mom loves riding too much to give it up even as she ages and...things happen."

"What about you, Madeline? Do you still love riding?"

"I don't know," Madeline said. "I haven't let myself think too much about it...until lately."

"What happened to your bike?"

"I sold it to get extra money for school. It was an easy choice, at the time, since I knew I wouldn't have much time for riding." Even to her own ears these reasons sounded powerless. Madeline hadn't needed extra money during her college days, and she knew she could've made time to ride. Her parents had encouraged her to do so, but bikes only reminded her of Scott and for so long she hadn't been ready to remember him.

She liked Gavin and getting reacquainted with motorcycles, but she wasn't ready to tell him what really happened with her bike. Even Madeline didn't know for sure. She'd told her parents to sell it, give it away, whatever. She didn't care.

"How about your endorsement?"

"I let it lapse when I sold the bike." Even as she said the words, Madeline was already thinking about getting the motorcycle operator's manual and brushing up so she could take the written test.

"With your experience you could get it back like that." Gavin snapped his fingers for emphasis. "Have you ever thought about getting another motorcycle?" he asked.

"Up until I rode with you on Tuesday and then again today, I thought I'd never want another bike. But now I'm actually opening to that idea." Madeline was surprised to hear herself admitting those words out loud.

"You can use my bike to refresh your skills," Gavin said.

"Whoa." Madeline held up a hand in protest, but the corners of her mouth lifted in a smile. "If, and I stress the 'if', I decide to ride again, it's probably better to practice on a smaller bike, like my mother's Sportster."

"If you can ride a Sportster, riding a bigger bike isn't that much different."

Madeline knew Gavin was right and yet she was anxious to turn the conversation away from motorcycles.

When their walk took them in front of a seafood restaurant, they stopped in their tracks, looking at each other.

"Are you hungry?" Gavin asked.

"Starving," Madeline said, "and seafood tops my list of favorites."

"That settles it," Gavin said. "We're going in."

Waiting to be seated, Gavin and Madeline continued their getting acquainted conversation.

"Do you have any brothers or sisters?" Gavin asked.

"No sisters. I had a brother...Scott. He died a long time ago in a motorcycle accident." Madeline's voice was barely audible.

"Madeline, I'm sorry."

"It's okay. I still have a brother."

"I'm confused. I thought you just had one brother," Gavin said.

"That's true," Madeline said. "I was thinking about Joe. We've known each other so long he seems like my brother."

"Got it," Gavin said, just as the hostess came by to seat them and for the time being their talk turned to menu choices.

When they had made their selections, Madeline looked across the table at Gavin and smiled.

"Cody looks so much like Scott did at that age, and I can tell the combination of adults and shiny motorcycles is as hard for him to resist as it was for my brother."

"Give yourself a chance to know Cody. He may resemble your brother, but he's a separate person."

"I know that," Madeline sighed. "It'll just take some time, that's all."

"I don't know much about you either, Gavin Marshall," Madeline continued, her eyes twinkling.

"Well, I'm a small-town, only child," Gavin said. "I was born in Heron's Cove and lived there until I graduated from high school. After that, I joined the Marine Corps and after I was discharged I wandered around for a while, then came back to Heron's Cove." He stopped a moment to acknowledge the waitress bringing their drinks. "After my mother died a few years ago, my dad moved to Florida but we're as close as that distance lets us be."

Madeline reached over to take his hand. "Tell me about your friendship with Dennis."

"Well, he's divorced, making him a single father with full custody of Cody."

"Is Cody's mom in the picture at all?" Madeline asked.

"Hasn't been for the past three years." Gavin's mouth drew back in a tight line. He remained silent for so long Madeline wondered if he would say anything else about Cody's mother.

"She's a drug addict. Spent the last two years in rehab and tells Denny she's clean." Gavin didn't look like he believed this. "Now she wants contact with Cody again."

"How does Cody feel about that?" Madeline asked.

Gavin shrugged. "He talks about her sometimes, but he doesn't really remember her."

"Does Cody have any pictures of his mother? They would help him remember her," Madeline said, only meaning to be helpful.

Gavin shoulders lifted and quickly fell. "I'm not sure Dennis wants Cody to remember her."

Privately Madeline thought this was wrong, but she felt a strong urge not to meddle.

"Has Dennis always lived in Heron's Cove?" Madeline asked, feeling it was safe to ask this question about him.

"No, he's originally from California. We met in Marine Corps boot camp. We fought in the first Gulf War together." Gavin shifted in his seat.

"You've been friends for a long time. Like me and Joe."

"Denny saved my life over there. I had my back turned and somebody lobbed a grenade that landed right by me. Denny saw what happened. He tackled me and forced me out of harm's way seconds before the grenade exploded." Madeline wondered what Gavin was thinking as a look of anguish crossed his face. While it was only there for a moment, Madeline sensed there was more to the story and longed to ease his pain.

"I think it's time for us to start on the dinner we're both hungry for," Gavin continued, seemingly relieved at the interruption provided by the arrival of their salads.

Madeline had little experience with military people and she'd never been told not to ask about what happened on a battlefield. But Gavin's relief at the appearance of their food sent her a signal to be quiet or at least to change the subject.

On their way back to the parking lot, Madeline said, "You may have to put more air in the tires in order for the bike to support us."

"I don't think that will be necessary." Gavin gave her shoulders a brief squeeze.

A few minutes after eight, Gavin and Madeline headed back to Heron's Cove. Being a passenger gave Madeline ample time to think, and after awhile she was surprised that none of her thoughts were about her brother's accident. Instead, she thought about how much Scott would have liked Gavin. *Well, little brother, that's something else we have in common.*

Though somewhat tired, Gavin and Madeline were charged up after the ride and the day together. Before they got off the bike Madeline wrapped her arms around Gavin's waist in a quick hug. He walked with her to the front door and waited while she unlocked it.

"Thank you for today, Gavin. It was incredible!" She turned to Gavin, taking both his hands in hers before stretching to kiss him on the cheek. "Would you like to come in?"

"I would, but I've got three jobs tomorrow, starting at nine, so I'd better be going."

Their gazes held for seconds before Gavin gently cupped Madeline's face in his hands and settled his lips lightly on hers, his kiss cautious and tender. He lingered there, savoring the feel of Madeline's skin against his, but he made no move to deepen the kiss.

When they pulled away, Gavin lifted one hand and brushed a strand of hair from Madeline's face.

"Goodnight, Ms. Spencer."

"Goodnight, Mr. Marshall."

Madeline stood on the porch, watching Gavin and his motorcycle grow smaller and smaller. *Maybe it's not so bad having a devil in my arms.* She pressed her fingertips to her mouth, hoping to somehow preserve the feel of Gavin's lips on hers. Now, finally, she knew what it felt like to be kissed by him. It was good, but too short. She wanted more.

Chapter Nine

When Madeline woke up Sunday morning, she recalled every detail of her day with Gavin. Except for the initial fright at the start of the ride, she hadn't enjoyed a day so thoroughly in years. The wind. The traffic. Coconut curry shrimp for dinner. Gavin's kiss. *If only that kiss had been longer.*

On that note, Madeline picked up the phone and punched in her mother's phone number. She quickly calculated what time it would be in England. Eight o'clock. A little late to be calling, but still okay. She wondered if her mother might be out. Whatever Sylvia Spencer was doing, Madeline knew she was having a good time.

"Hi, Mom," Madeline said when one of her mother's friends picked up on the fourth ring. "Oh sorry. This is Madeline." She listened to the music playing in the background, waiting for her mother to come on the line.

"You sound chipper this morning, Madeline, but I guess you should considering it's almost noon. Late night?"

"As a matter of fact, it was, and a good one at that." Madeline settled in for the conversation already feeling her mother's smile. "But let me tell you about Friday first. You'll never guess what I did, Mom. It was awesome!"

"I give. What did you do?"

"You know I don't have much hands-on experience with large animals, right?"

"Yes. If I recall, you were always scared of horses and cows. Though how you could be, with Joe for a friend, I'll never know."

"Well, I went out with Joe to a farm that raises Arabian horses. One of the mares was having a problem delivering and we assisted. I actually played an active part in delivering the foal, Mom. Joe thought the change of pace would be invigorating for me, and he was right. I really accomplished something."

"I take it mare and foal are okay?"

"They're absolutely perfect."

"You're enjoying this, aren't you?" Sylvia asked.

"You mean working with Joe and helping with the horses? Of course I am."

"No. I mean the way you're avoiding telling me about your late night."

"Mom! I am not."

"Good. Now tell me about what has you sounding so ready to take on the world."

"I spent the day in Portland."

"Oh." Sylvia's disappointment snaked through the phone wires to Madeline's ears. "That's exciting."

"Wait, Mom, there's more. I went there and back on a motorcycle."

"It must be the long distance connection. I thought you just said you rode a bike."

"I did say that, Mom."

"Did you buy another one?"

"No, not yet. I rode as a passenger. In fact, in the last week, I've been on two motorcycle rides."

"Twice?"

"Yes. If I can spare the time tomorrow, I'll go down to the DMV and get the motorcycle operator's manual so I can study for the written test."

"It's about time you got back to riding." Madeline could hear the smile in her mother's voice. "Okay, I know you didn't ride with Joe. Tell me about whoever was responsible for changing your mind. I want to meet him." There was a pause that had nothing to do with the long distance connection. "It is a him, isn't it?"

"Yes, Mom. It's a him. His name is Gavin Marshall, the guy Joe recommended to take care of my yard. I will make sure you get a chance to meet him when you come down. Are you riding down here?"

"If the weather even partially holds, you bet I will. I'm not a rain chicken like you."

Madeline and her mom said their goodbyes and

Madeline started thinking about what to fix for dinner. She knew one thing for sure.

****

On his way home after his last job on Sunday, Gavin stopped by Dennis's house. Cody was playing with a friend down the street so Gavin didn't get a chance to visit with him.

"Got a call from Paula this afternoon," Dennis said, grabbing two cans of beer from the fridge.

"What did she want this time?" Gavin asked. He couldn't stifle his intense dislike for the woman who had caused his best friend so much pain.

"Says she's coming down for Cody's birthday."

"I'm surprised she could even remember it," Gavin said.

"Yeah. Me, too."

"Did she talk to Cody?" Gavin asked.

"She wanted to, but I told her he was at a friend's house. In fact, he's still there. Spent last night with his friend." Dennis stopped to take a long drink of the beer he had been looking at. "Anyway, she thought I was lying to keep her and Cody apart. Things got pretty ugly and I hung up. I wasn't lying, Gavin, but..."

"You do want to keep them apart."

"Boy, do I ever," Dennis said.

Gavin and Dennis enjoyed their beer and for a while neither of them made any attempt to interrupt the silence guys can fall into so easily.

"So how'd you get hooked up with the doc?" Dennis was the first one to break the silence.

"Doc?" Gavin sat there with a blank look on his face.

"You know who I'm talking about," Dennis said. "The pretty lady who helped rescue Mako."

"We are not hooked up." Gavin clipped the words, making each one sound like a separate sentence.

Dennis eyed his friend closely. "Sorry. It was just an expression, man."

"I know," Gavin said. "But we aren't, as you put it, hooked up. Joe recommended me to take care of Madeline's lawn. That's what I'll do."

"You've got it bad, my friend," Dennis said, looking

across the table at Gavin.

"What are you talking about?" Gavin asked.

"Madeline. You're falling for her."

"You're not even close to being right." Gavin took a long swig of his beer, hating the fact his best friend saw straight through him.

This time it wasn't an easy masculine silence that built up between them. It was rough, like Dennis and Gavin themselves.

"Just be careful, buddy," Dennis finally said. "Don't go down any dead-end roads." As if fearing he might have said too much, he changed the subject. "Cody's birthday party is all set up for Saturday afternoon at Murphy's Pizza. Don't forget."

"I won't." With that, Gavin drained the last of his second beer and left.

He thought about Dennis's words all the way home. He knew Dennis had been talking about Amy. Boy, had that been a dead-end road. But Madeline was nothing like Amy.

Or is there a chance Dennis is right? Gavin figured Madeline grew up rich and privileged. Hell, she was still rich. There is nothing I can offer her except my services as a yard-worker. *None of that matters, I'm just in her life to take of her yard. That's all.*

In spite of this line of thinking, Gavin called Madeline as soon as he had showered. He couldn't wait to hear her voice again even if it was just over the phone.

"Hi, Madeline."

"Hi. I'll bet you're tired after working all day."

"Actually, I'm not," Gavin said and then rushed into the invitation. "Cody's birthday is Saturday and Denny's planned a party at Murphy's. Would you like to come? It would mean a lot to Cody." He was aware of Madeline's slight hesitation and hoped she wouldn't say no.

"Sure. I know Cody loves motorcycles, but he already has everything except the bike. What else is he interested in?"

"Sharks." Gavin answered readily. "The kid loves sharks."

"Okay," Madeline said. "I'll look for something shark

related."

"You don't have to buy him anything," Gavin said.

"I know, but I...um...I want to."

"Would you like to do something tonight? Maybe go out to dinner?"

"Gavin, I'd love to, but I've invited Joe over for dinner. Why don't you join us?"

"Thanks anyway, I don't want to intrude. I'll see you at Cody's party."

Keen disappointment hit Gavin when he hung up the phone. So this is how it's going to be. I'm only an afterthought in Madeline Spencer's life. Gavin told himself he didn't have a right to expect anything else.

Gavin may have been disappointed, but he was also in the mood to party. So what if it was Sunday? He'd worked hard and he wanted to have some fun. If Madeline Spencer was unwilling, no matter. Gavin knew plenty of women who would be willing.

He began to reach for his cell phone before some stiffness caused him to remember his work that day. Some days managing two jobs, especially with one of them being landscaping, just seemed like a lot of hassle. Maybe it was time to slow down a bit.

Now Gavin recalled the conversation he had two years ago with his friend, Bill, about fishing in Alaska. They had grown up together; only Bill had left as soon as he graduated from high school. He told Gavin he felt like the little town was strangling him.

On his last trip back, though, Bill had ridden down from Seattle on a motorcycle that sounded like it needed some work.

"Bill, sounds like your machine is running a little rough." Gavin had to give his friend a hard time.

"Yeah, I was hoping you would take a look at it for me," Bill said. "I was never as good as you when it came to working on bike engines."

Gavin clapped his friend on the back.

"Sure, Bill, I'll check it out after we've done some catching up."

Gavin pulled two beers from the fridge and they went out to sit in the backyard.

"Your yard is looking good," Bill had told Gavin. "I don't understand how you manage it and still work full-time."

Gavin laughed. "I've given up my free time and any semblance of a social life."

"You still plan to open your landscaping business?" Bill asked.

"Yes, I do," Gavin said. "I could open it now, but it would be nice if I had a little more of a financial cushion before I quit my job."

Bill took a long swig of his beer before he spoke again. "I think I might be able to help you out."

"What are you talking about?" Gavin asked. "I didn't know you were rich enough to float me a loan."

Now it was Bill's turn to laugh. "No, what I have in mind is a fishing trip."

"I don't see how that is going to help me open any kind of business."

"I'm talking about fishing in Alaska this summer for a couple of months. You know I've been going up there every summer for the last ten years, right? Anyway, this is where you come in. My friend needs one more person to round out his crew. You interested?"

Gavin pondered what Bill had told him. He went inside and returned with two more beers.

"That depends," he said, popping the tops on the bottles. "I'm not crazy about being on the water. How big is the boat?"

"Oh, it's huge, thirty-two foot long. Sleeps four of us."

"Bill, have you lost your mind?" Gavin asked. "A thirty-two foot boat isn't what I'd call huge. And a crew of four? That makes it even smaller. This isn't for me."

"Don't be so quick to turn it down, Gavin. You could make quite a bit of money if the fishing is good."

Gavin had turned down Bill's offer. Now he wondered if going to Alaska might be a good thing for him, but at the same time he knew that running away wouldn't erase what he felt for Madeline.

I have to get my mind off of her. He flipped open his phone and dialed the number for Barb Conley.

"Hey, baby." Barb had Caller ID. "What's going on?"

"You up for a good time, Toots?" Gavin asked.

"Always with you. I get off work in an hour."

"Good. I'll pick you up then."

Gavin snapped his phone shut. His night was set. This little electronic black-book was priceless.

He picked Barb up when she got off work and they rode to her place. Somehow, on the bike, Barb managed to hold on to the cartons of Chinese takeout.

"You're spending the night, aren't you?" Barb asked, finishing her last bite of fried rice and leaning into Gavin. Her hand stroked the inside of his leg before finally stopping on the bulge threatening to break free of the confining jeans.

Gavin growled, a sound not unlike a Harley engine at full throttle. "If you don't stop what you're doing, I won't have a choice," he said, taking her face in his hands and crushing her lips in a hard, demanding kiss.

Gavin and Barb worked their way to her bedroom, leaving a varied trail of clothing in their wake.

****

Madeline was just about ready for her dinner with Joe. The night before she had chopped and marinated ingredients for the garden pasta salad to be served with grilled steaks and baked potatoes.

At four-thirty, Joe pulled up in the driveway. After getting out, he reached into the backseat and pulled out a large cake box.

"Joe, is that what I think it is?"

"It's a German chocolate cake. Your favorite. Sorry, but I didn't make this one from scratch." Joe handed the box to Maddy before taking a seat. "Maddy, you scared me the other day when you threatened to bring a vegetable tray to work instead of doughnuts."

"I baked a pecan pie. *Your* favorite," Madeline said, emphasizing the your.

"Excellent," Joe said. "I can take home half the pie and I'll leave half the cake."

Madeline just shook her head.

"Did I tell you Mom is coming down for a visit?" Madeline asked when they were piling the extra goodies on their baked potatoes.

"No, you didn't. When is she coming and how long is she staying?"

"Next Saturday. I don't know how long she will be here."

"This is just too good," Joe said, satisfied at last with his heaping plate. "You have to introduce her to Gavin."

"I was planning to. I invited him over tonight but he said he didn't want to intrude. My guess is he'll probably say the same thing when Mom gets here."

"Give him another chance, Maddy. We'll have a huge party when Mom gets here. A block party." Joe looked like a little kid planning his birthday party. "That's the ticket. The 4th of July is just around the corner."

It was true. Those gaudy yellow fireworks stands were popping up all over Heron's Cove, a sure indication the 4th was close at hand.

A look of doubt popped across Joe's face, "She'll be here on the 3rd. Do you think she will be too tired for a party?"

"Are you kidding? Sometimes I think Mom is the original party animal," Madeline said.

This brought more cheer to Joe's face. "I can't wait until she gets here."

After the dishes had been cleared, Madeline and Joe sat on the back deck, enjoying coffee, cake and pecan pie.

"Are you sleeping okay these days?"

"You know something, Joe? I haven't had any nightmares since I moved here. Just the stupid kinds of dreams that make no sense at all."

"Especially since you rode with Gavin?"

"Yes, especially since I rode with Gavin." Madeline's own love for motorcycles was being slowly reawakened and she realized she had Gavin to thank for that.

"I am so happy for you, Maddy." Madeline knew Joe had long been concerned about her recurring nightmares so she truly felt his concern and caring.

"I only wish Scott could have met Gavin."

"He approves. He's looking down and smiling. You know that, don't you?"

"Yeah, I do, Joe, but I still wish they could've met face to face. There's something else."

"What's that?"

"I told Gavin about Scott's accident, but he doesn't know yet that I was there."

"You are going to tell him, right?"

"Yes, Joe, I am."

"Maddy, you've made so much progress just since you moved down here. I always believed that when you were ready to let it, the healing process would take over."

"I'm getting better, Joe." Madeline smiled. " But, I'm not cured yet."

She could see that her comments did nothing to shake Joe's faith. "You will be."

When Joe went home, Madeline called Gavin, but her call went to voicemail so she left a message.

"It's me. Madeline. I just wanted you to know you wouldn't have been intruding tonight. After all, Joe introduced us. Um, call me when you get a chance."

Madeline hung up and curled up in bed with a book. When she got Gavin's voicemail, Madeline couldn't help but picture him out carousing with some other woman. She tried reasoning with herself, but she couldn't restrain the sharp little fingers of...what...jealousy? *I have no claim on Gavin. What's it to me who he runs around with?*

****

Sometime in the early hours of Monday morning, Gavin got out of Barb's bed, dressed and rode home. When he walked in the door, he looked at his phone and saw he had a message. Just hearing Madeline's voice was enough to send a surge of desire sweeping over him, immediately replaced by a feeling of doubt.

Looks like I'm just a passing reflection in her eyes.

He crawled into his own bed, but he knew it would be a long time before he got to sleep. More than anything he wanted to call Madeline, to apologize for being with Barb, but it was too early to call.

In that moment Gavin knew he was willing to take a big step on what Dennis called a dead-end road, especially if it meant being with Madeline. The realization both terrified and thrilled him.

Chapter Ten

Monday brought Madeline two surprises, both of them welcome.

Joe was out tending to an equine patient while Madeline and Kelly were taking advantage of the temporary lull to enjoy coffee in the break room.

"Isn't it funny that it's 85 degrees outside and we're in here drinking hot coffee?" Madeline was ready to refill her cup.

"Try putting an ice cube in it like I did," Kelly said.

"Smart girl." Madeline sat down with her newly filled cup of hot coffee.

"Um, Madeline, Joe asked me out Friday." Kelly kept her eyes lowered.

"Kelly, that is so cool. Good for the both of you." Madeline was truly pleased for the younger woman. Kelly's personality had been key to Madeline's smooth adjustment at the hospital.

It delighted Madeline to hear Joe was finding some personal happiness. *After the tremendous help Joe has been to me, he deserves to be happy in his own life.*

"Did Joe say anything to you?" Kelly asked.

"As a matter of fact, he didn't. Has he got some explaining to do!" Madeline couldn't stop herself as she started laughing.

"What's so funny?"

"Nothing, really," Madeline said, regaining control of herself. "It's just Joe never hesitates to ask questions about my personal life, but when it comes to his, well, all I get is one or two word answers."

"I know what you mean," Kelly said. "Women are always ready to talk. About anything. Why is that?"

"I don't know," Madeline took a sip of her now cooling coffee. "Where are you and Joe going?"

"Out to dinner at the new steakhouse."

"I haven't been there yet so let me know how it is."

"Okay. Maybe you and Gavin can have dinner there next." Kelly grinned.

Madeline feigned shock at her assistant's suggestion and tossed a crumpled paper towel at her.

"It's really okay with you if I go out with Joe?" Kelly once again turned serious.

"Of course it's all right. Why do you even ask?"

"Well, you and Joe are so close and I thought..." Kelly's voice abandoned her.

"You thought there was something between me and Joe." Recognition dawned on Madeline. "Kelly, you thought wrong. Joe and I have known each other since junior high school. He's my best friend and I love him dearly. But I love him like a brother. It's like I grew up with two brothers. By all means go out with him. You deserve to be happy and so does Joe."

Joe walked into the break room just then, effectively stopping the conversation between Madeline and Kelly.

"So does Joe what?" he asked, looking around, probably for doughnuts.

Kelly pushed back from the table, nearly upending her chair. She almost ran back to her desk.

"Nothing you need to worry about," Madeline assured him, moving away from the table.

The second surprise of the day came when Madeline walked into the clinic after lunch. The first thing she noticed was the bouquet of a dozen yellow roses on the front office counter.

"Wow! Who got flowers?" Madeline asked, feeling her already high spirits soar even higher. She didn't even stop to consider that the flowers were for her.

"Well, they aren't mine." Kelly wore an odd little grin. "And I'm pretty sure nobody would send flowers to Joe. Guess that leaves you, Madeline." She pretended to concentrate on a file open on her desk.

Madeline plucked the small envelope from its place in the middle of the roses and removed the card. It simply read, "Love, Gavin." She was suddenly light-headed. Did the word "love" on the card carry significant meaning or had Gavin used it in a generic way. *Love isn't generic, Madeline.* That voice again!

"You knew all the time, didn't you?" Madeline handed the card to Kelly who had given up all pretense of working.

"Oh, Madeline, this is so romantic. I knew the roses were for you because the delivery guy said he had flowers for Madeline Spencer. But I didn't know they were from Gavin. I swear, I didn't read the card."

"Relax, Kelly. I believe you." Madeline dialed Gavin's cell phone but it went directly to his voicemail. She was too busy the remainder of the day to notice he didn't return her call.

****

Gavin and Dennis got surprised on Monday, too, but in a potentially sinister way. It all started when Dennis got off work and picked Cody up at his daycare center. When they got home, Cody freed Mako from his cage.

"Dad, can I take Mako outside?"

"Yes, but only until I get out of the shower and get dressed. Then you'll have to come inside to get washed up for dinner."

"Okay. Is Gavin coming over for dinner?"

"I don't know, Cody."

Cody was in the front yard with Mako on his shoulder when a late-model, dark green sedan pulled up to the curb in front of his house.

The woman got out of her car not believing her good luck. *It can't possibly be this easy.*

"Hello," she said.

"Hi." Cody, gregarious by nature, was eager to talk. In that moment he forgot he wasn't supposed to talk to strangers.

"What's your name?"

"Cody."

This is even easier than I thought it would be. The information I got was dead on and the pieces are falling in place almost faster than I can keep up with them.

"That's a mighty big bird for such a little boy to be carrying around," she said.

"I'm not a little boy," Cody said. "I'm big. Dad calls

me his little man." Cody stretched on his tiptoes, trying to impress the woman with his size.

"Of course you're not a little boy. I'm sorry if I hurt your feelings."

"That's okay," Cody told her, the insult forgotten. "My birthday is Saturday. I'll be seven. We're having a party at Murphy's Pizza."

"I hope you have a great birthday. Is that your bird?"

"It's my dad's bird. His name's Mako. My dad's name is Dennis."

"Won't the bird fly away?"

"No. Madeline cut his wings."

"Who's Madeline?" the woman asked.

"She's a doctor," Cody said. "A veteri..." Cody struggled with the word.

"Oh, she's a veterinarian."

"Yeah, that's it." Cody grinned.

"Can I take your picture with that beautiful bird?" The woman took a small disposable camera out of her pocket.

"Sure," Cody said, always ready to pose.

****

Gavin pulled into the driveway just as the woman hastily stuffed the camera back in her pocket.

"Uncle Gavin!" Cody ran over to Gavin's bike, Mako bouncing on his shoulder, doing his best to keep his balance.

"Who are you talking to, buddy?" Gavin ruffled Cody's hair.

"That lady." Cody pointed to the woman standing on the sidewalk, watching the exchange between Gavin and Cody. "She took my picture."

"Do you know who she is?" Gavin asked.

"No." Cody's voice was suddenly very small. He sensed trouble coming.

"Go inside, Cody."

Cody didn't say anything, nor did he move.

"Cody. Inside." Although Gavin didn't raise his voice, the effect of his tone was immediate. Cody ran inside, tears streaming down his cheeks.

Gavin walked over to where the woman stood.

"I don't know who you are and I don't care. It's time for you to go, but before you do, hand over that camera."

"I-I don't know what you're talking about," the woman said.

"Bullshit. The camera I saw you put in your pocket. You have no right taking the kid's picture. Hand over the camera." Gavin advanced on the woman, his hand outstretched. "Now."

The woman shrunk back toward her car, never taking her eyes from Gavin's face.

"Give me the goddamn camera," Gavin demanded.

The woman was completely aware of Gavin's imposing figure. She handed over the camera and got in her car without a word. *You might not care who I am now, but you'll care before long. And so will Dennis.* True, she had lost the camera, but she could always take more pictures at the birthday party. The fact she wasn't invited didn't bother the woman at all. She was too elated at how easily all the pieces of this fractured picture were realigning, with little effort required on her part.

****

Dennis came out of the bathroom, toweling his hair, just in time to see Cody disappear into his room with Gavin close behind.

"What's going on?" Dennis asked, tossing the towel back in the bathroom.

"Cody was outside just now talking to a strange woman. Told me he didn't know who she was." Gavin struggled to keep his voice and his breathing even. "Just as I rode up she took a few steps in Cody's direction."

"I'll go talk to him." Dennis started down the hall to his son's room.

"I'm going with you," Gavin said.

"He's my kid." Dennis's voice was hard and he didn't look back at his friend. "I'll handle it."

"I know Cody's your kid and I know you don't need my help dealing with him. But I made him cry and I need to explain why I did that."

Dennis offered no further resistance as he and Gavin walked down the hall to Cody's room.

They stopped just outside Cody's room. He hadn't

83

closed his door all the way and they could see him laying face down on the bed, shaking with sobs. Gavin knocked.

"Hey, little buddy, can we come in?" Gavin asked.

Cody didn't answer.

"Cody? We're coming in," Dennis said. He hesitated only a moment, then pushed the door open the rest of the way.

Gavin sat down on the bed beside Cody while Dennis stood at the head of the bed.

"I'm sorry I made you cry," Gavin said, putting his hand on the little boy's shoulder. "But I got real scared when I saw you talking to that lady."

"Why?" Cody asked, wiping an arm across his face.

"Because she was a stranger and I was afraid she might try to take you away."

"I wouldn't let her 'cause I love Daddy and I love you, too."

It was a little while before Gavin could force words around the lump in his throat.

"Are you still my big buddy?" Cody asked.

"You better believe it. Gimme five," Gavin said.

Cody and Gavin exchanged high fives and Gavin left the room.

Dennis walked over and sat down beside his son.

"It's true what Gavin said? You were talking to a stranger?"

"Yes, Dad," Cody said, his voice small and low.

"What did she say?"

"She said Mako was a big bird."

"Did she say anything else?" Dennis fervently hoped his son hadn't divulged personal information like phone numbers or last names. He wondered who this woman was and exactly what she had wanted.

"She thought he could fly away but I told her Madeline cut his wings."

"Did she ask you anything?"

"What my name was. I told her it was Cody. And, and I told her your name was Dennis." Fresh tears spilled down Cody's cheeks.

"What have we told you about talking to strangers?" Dennis indicated himself and gestured to where Gavin had been standing.

"Don't do it." Cody's answer was swift.

"That's right," Dennis said. "What should you do if a stranger tries to talk to you again?"

"I should tell you or Uncle Gavin. Or go in the house. Am I grounded?"

"Do you think you should be?" Dennis asked.

Cody meekly nodded.

"Okay. No motorcycle rides for a week. Do we have a deal?" Dennis knew the no riding deal would make more of an impression on his son than anything else.

"Yes, Dad."

"Don't ever do this again."

"I won't, Dad. I promise."

"Dad?"

"Yes, Cody?"

"Can I ride to my party on Saturday?" Cody wasn't entirely sure how long a week was.

"I don't know, son. I can't answer that right now. Let me think about it. Now go wash up for dinner."

Cody knew better than to press his father about riding.

"Yes, sir," he told his dad and headed for the bathroom.

Gavin and Dennis walked outside and Dennis sat on the back steps while Gavin walked over to the garbage can ready to drop the camera inside.

"What's that?" Dennis asked.

Gavin looked down at the camera as if seeing it for the first time. "She took Cody's picture. I saw her jam the camera in her pocket just as I rode up."

"I see you persuaded her to give it up," Dennis said. "Don't toss it. Maybe there's something on it that will help us figure out who she is."

"I'll drop it off to be developed on my way home," Gavin said.

"What the hell happened out front tonight?" Dennis asked.

"I don't know, but my guts froze when that woman started walking toward Cody. Maybe it was innocent, maybe she only stopped because she wanted a closer look at Mako." Gavin sounded for the entire world like he didn't believe a word of what he had just said.

"I don't believe that for a minute," Dennis said.

"Neither do I. Hell, I was so pissed I didn't think about getting the license plate number. My only concern was making sure Cody was safe."

"Why do you suppose Cody talked to her in the first place? He knows better." Dennis thumped the deck for emphasis.

"You know how much he loves that bird and how much he loves to talk. He was probably flattered when she noticed Mako on his shoulder. Made Cody feel like big stuff."

"Did you recognize her at all?"

Gavin shook his head.

"I'd been home for less than fifteen minutes and Cody handles Mako all the time. He was in his own yard and..." Dennis rambled until he ran out of words. In the end he sat on the steps with his hands dangling between his knees.

"Hey, man," Gavin said, "you didn't do anything wrong."

"But what if it happens again? With that woman or someone else?"

"You and I are going to do everything we can to see that it doesn't," Gavin said.

****

Madeline still hadn't heard from Gavin when she left work for the day, but she figured he was probably as busy as she was. While she was waiting for her pasta to cook, she reread the card that had been tucked in with the flowers. *Does this change anything between us? Or am I reading too much into his signature?*

She was halfway through dinner at seven o'clock when the phone rang.

"Hello?"

"Hi, Madeline. I'm sorry I didn't call you back earlier, but we had a little situation with Cody. I haven't gone home yet."

"Is Cody all right?" Madeline asked.

"Yeah, everything's cool. *Now.* I don't want to talk

about it on the phone. I'll tell you all about it the next time I see you."

"I understand," Madeline said. "The flowers are beautiful, Gavin. Thank you so much."

"I'm glad you like them. I meant the flowers to say thanks for Saturday, too. I wouldn't have enjoyed the ride nearly as much if you hadn't been with me. Come to think about it, I probably wouldn't have gone if you had said no."

"You helped me whether you realize it or not. I used to love riding and now, thanks to you, I'm starting to again. I picked up the motorcycle manual today so I can study for the written test."

"Good for you. My offer to use my bike is still good."

"I appreciate that, Gavin, I really do. But since I haven't ridden in so long I think it's best if I start off with a smaller bike. Would you like to stop by on your way home?"

"I would, but I'm so tired I'd probably fall asleep on your doorstep," Gavin said.

"Gavin, you really wouldn't have been intruding Sunday when I had Joe over for dinner. I didn't mean it to sound like an afterthought invitation."

"I know," Gavin said, his voice quiet.

"Would you like to come over for dinner tomorrow night?" Madeline asked. "That is if you don't have other plans."

"Unless work interferes, I don't have any plans," Gavin said. "What time?"

"Why don't you come over around six? I'll make a salad tomorrow before I go to work and I'll grill burgers. With the weather this fantastic, I can't bear the thought of cooking inside."

"Sounds good," Gavin said. "Can I bring anything?"

"No," Madeline said. "Just yourself and your appetite."

"Okay, I'll see you tomorrow night. Goodnight, Madeline."

"Goodnight, Gavin."

"I...Good-night, Madeline." Gavin repeated his goodnight.

Madeline wondered if Gavin had really been about to say I love you. *Maybe when he signed the card "Love, Gavin" he just meant love as a generic expression, part of his signature.*

Chapter Eleven

Madeline set the small table in the breakfast nook. It was close to the back deck where the grill was, making it convenient to serve the meal. She stood back, wondering if the two candles she had selected were appropriate to use for a centerpiece. Kelly was right; Gavin's sending the roses had been a romantic gesture. Exhaling noisily, she jerked the candleholders from the table. Was candlelight over the top for grilled burgers and salad? Madeline decided she didn't care. She loved candles so she decided to use one candle in a wine bottle set to one side of the table—visible but not the focal point. It was more fitting with her planned menu. "I really have to give the bottle back to Joe, but not tonight," Madeline said out loud, sticking the candle in the bottle.

Just then her phone rang and Madeline hoped it wasn't Gavin.

"Hello."

"Dr. Spencer?" the male voice questioned.

"Yes," Madeline answered.

"It's Mr. Evans."

"What can I do for you, Mr. Evans?"

"I've decided to sell the house. You told me you might be interested in buying so I'm giving you the first chance before I put it on the market."

"I see," Madeline said, stalling for some time to think about whether she really wanted to buy the house.

"Don't worry," Mr. Evans said hastily. "You don't have to give me an answer right now. I know it's kinda sudden and all."

"Thank you for the call, Mr. Evans," Madeline felt relieved that he was giving her some time. "Can I give you my answer by the end of the week?"

"Sure, sure."

As she reviewed the call in her mind after hanging up, Madeline could tell Mr. Evans hadn't been pleased at her ambivalent response, and she didn't trust him not to list the house anyway. She wondered briefly if negotiating a sales price would be as tough as doing their current lease agreement.

When Madeline heard the motorcycle, she came out on the porch. "Hi, Gavin." She didn't try to conceal the delight she felt. In all honesty, delight wasn't all she felt. Tension swept through her. The fire burning low in her body had nothing to do with the outside temperature. The tension built as she watched Gavin take the steps two at a time to where she stood on the porch. His kiss only stoked the craving she felt.

"Hi, Madeline. Do I have time to take your neighbor for a ride?" Gavin asked.

Madeline looked at her watch. She had made the salad before she went to work this morning; all that remained to be done was slicing the lettuce, tomatoes and pickles. "Sure. I'll start grilling the burgers when you get back."

****

Gavin was looking forward to this excursion with Madeline's neighbor and was pleased with his welcome.

"Angel! This is a surprise. Come in." Emma held the door open.

"Thanks, but I came over to ask if you'd like to go for a ride."

"Now? Well, I suppose so. I don't have any gear, though."

"Not to worry," Gavin said. "Madeline borrowed some from a friend of mine and you can borrow it from Madeline. Do you have a pair of jeans?"

Emma pretended disdain. "Angel, I've not owned a pair of jeans in my life."

"Well, then, you can wear a pair of Madeline's." Gavin offered his arm, which Emma readily accepted.

It wasn't long before Emma was outfitted in all her borrowed gear. Madeline's jeans were a bit large for her so a belt was needed to hold them in place around her waist. Gavin taped the legs of the jeans around her ankles so they wouldn't get caught on anything. Madeline came out to help Emma get on the bike, but Gavin had everything under control.

Twenty minutes after they left, Gavin and his passenger returned. Once they reached the driveway and came to a stop, Gavin helped his passenger dismount.

"So how was it, my fair lady."

"Angel, that was terrifying."

Gavin immediately felt for her. "Oh, Emma, I'm sorry..."

Her laughter interrupted him, "To be honest, that was the most exciting thing I have done in years. You are a dear to have given this old woman's heart such joy; I had almost forgotten how much fun it can be to ride like the wind."

Gavin had to laugh at the sheer joy shown on Emma's face.

****

"How was the ride?" Madeline asked, noting the shine in the old woman's eyes.

"I was terrified, to start." Emma didn't look at all terrified now.

The three of them went inside and Emma divested herself of the loaned gear. "I'll launder your jeans and return them tomorrow, dear," she said to Madeline.

"There's no hurry," Madeline said. "Would you like to join us for dinner?"

"Good heavens, no. I've got to go home and call my daughter. She won't believe what I just did. Goodnight, Madeline. Goodnight, Angel."

Gavin and Madeline breathed a collective, though silent, sigh of relief at Emma's refusal. They definitely wanted this night to themselves.

"I'll walk you home," Gavin said.

"What did she really think of the ride?" Madeline asked when Gavin came back a few minutes later.

"She was pretty scared at first; hung on tighter than you did. But on the way back I distinctly heard a couple of whoops."

"You got another one, Mr. Marshall."

"Another one?" Gavin looked puzzled.

"Yes. You reintroduced me to riding, or have you forgotten already?" Madeline smiled.

"No, I haven't forgotten at all," Gavin said.

Over dinner Madeline asked Gavin about the incident with Cody.

"You said you and Dennis had a situation with Cody yesterday. What happened?" Madeline asked. "Is he all right?" In spite of her resolve not to, she was getting attached to the little boy.

"Cody is fine. But I stopped by yesterday on my way home from work to find him outside with Mako on his shoulder, talking to a strange woman. Just as I rode up she was walking toward him. Cody said she took his picture. I got scared and told Cody to go inside, which made him cry. Then I told that woman to move on, but not before I took her camera away."

"It's understandable why you got scared, Gavin. A lot of kids are snatched by people meaning to do them harm. Did Cody know who she was?"

"When I asked him who he was talking to, he pointed and said 'that lady', so I don't think he knew her. Cody knows he's not supposed to talk to strangers," Gavin continued. "Why did he do it yesterday?"

"He's almost seven, so yes, he is old enough to know better. But he is still a little boy, Gavin, and little kids can't be counted on to remember all the lessons we teach them."

"The bird undoubtedly drew the woman's attention; maybe that's why she stopped. The whole encounter was probably innocent." Gavin hadn't believed this earlier and Madeline wasn't sure she believed it now.

"How did Dennis react?" Madeline asked.

"He blames himself, I think, for not keeping a closer eye on Cody. He was in the shower when it happened and he knew Cody was outside with the bird."

"Dennis didn't do anything wrong," Madeline said.

"That's what I told him, but he didn't really believe me."

"What did you do with the camera?" Madeline asked.

"I was about to toss it in the garbage can when Dennis stopped me. He said maybe there was something in there that could help us identify the mystery woman."

"Was there?" Madeline asked.

"No. Evidently she only had time to take a couple pictures before I showed up."

While Gavin and Madeline put away the food and loaded the dishwasher, the talk turned once more to motorcycles.

"Do you mind talking about Scott?" Gavin asked.

"Not at all." Madeline answered without hesitation. "What would you like to know?"

"Well, anything you care to tell me."

"He was three years younger than me and a charmer from the beginning. It was difficult to deny him anything."

"Were you jealous of Scott?" Gavin asked.

"God, no," Madeline said. "I think I was his biggest supporter, and later on, his biggest fan."

"Fan?" Gavin looked puzzled.

"Yes. Scott was into racing. Let me back up a bit." Madeline turned to face Gavin. "I started riding when I was five and racing when I was ten. Scott, on the other hand, started riding when he was six and in a year he was racing."

"Motocross or flat track?" Gavin asked.

"Flat track. Both of us."

"It's not too late," Gavin said. "Maybe you can start racing again."

"Not a chance," Madeline said. "That is definitely a young person's game. I quit racing when I was fifteen. Decided I wanted to concentrate on studying and I didn't think I could do justice to racing or school work if I kept trying to do both. I wasn't any good at racing anyway. Scott kept with it and he was awesome. When he was just riding he wasn't a hot dog as we all saw to that, but when he was on the track he was all about racing as hard as he could."

Madeline continued her journey down memory lane. "If it had been up to Scott, he wouldn't have done anything but race. Mom and Dad insisted good grades came first, racing second. Scott didn't have a choice, if he wanted to race, he had to keep his grades up to a high standard. He did, too, never bringing home less than a B on his report cards."

A memory of that slipping grade in English poked its way into Madeline's thoughts, but she wasn't about to share that with Gavin. That would mean telling him the real reason Scott had died in that horrible accident.

"You said your brother was killed in a motorcycle accident. Can you talk about it?"

Madeline heard nothing but compassion in Gavin's voice and found she was indeed ready to answer his question. But she also realized she wasn't ready to share why she felt the accident had been her fault. The bare bones of the story would have to do for now.

"Scott was riding his bike and I was on my own. A drunk driver rear-ended Scott's motorcycle, killing him instantly. I was riding behind him and saw the whole thing. I never rode again after that."

Gavin drew a deep breath and exhaled forcefully as though in doing so he could blow away the bad image Madeline carried. "So when you rode with us last Tuesday it the first time you had been on a motorcycle since the accident?"

"Yes, it was. Joe has told me more than once that it's time I get on with my life and I think he is right. Riding is a big step in that direction."

Madeline put in some soft jazz CDs and then settled herself on the couch. Gavin was about to join her when he noticed the motorcycle manual lying on the coffee table. He picked it up and flipped it open about midway.

"Okay, how much stopping power does the front brake have?"

"That's easy," Madeline told him. "Three-quarters. Ask me something else."

Gavin combed through the book, as though searching for a harder question.

"What should you do if your motorcycle starts to wobble?"

"Well, if you're carrying a load, lighten it if you can. If not, shift the load around so it's lower and further forward on the bike. Make sure the tire pressure, air shocks and dampers are set for the weight you are carrying. Fairings and windshield, if you have them, should be mounted properly."

Madeline found she could continue easily. "Don't accelerate out of a wobble. That only makes the bike more unstable. Take a firm hold on the handlebars and close the throttle gradually to slow down."

"You have been studying." Gavin was impressed.

"Yes, but a lot of it is rushing back to me from all those years ago." Madeline smiled. "Now, Mr. Marshall, ask me a hard question."

Gavin closed the book and returned it to the coffee table.

"A man and a beautiful woman have dinner, a dinner she made for him. There's a candle in a Chianti bottle in the middle of the table. The candle is lit and the wax drips down the neck of the bottle. The man and woman talk and eat, all the while watching each other over the candlelight."

Madeline sat mesmerized as he continued, "After dinner they relax on the couch. There's soft music playing in the background. The drapes are drawn across the living room windows and there's a bouquet of yellow roses on the coffee table. They turn to each other and then...?" Gavin left the question suspended between them.

Madeline, enjoying the soft fire spreading through her body, moved closer to Gavin and put her hand on his leg.

Gavin cupped Madeline's chin in one hand and lowered his head until his mouth covered hers. This time his kiss was neither cautious nor gentle. His desire revealed itself in the way he crushed her lips with his.

They parted briefly.

"Good answer, Ms. Spencer." Gavin then cupped the back of Madeline's head in his right hand, his fingers twisting in her hair. His left hand, on her waist, pulled her closer to him. When he sought to further part Madeline's lips with his tongue, she eagerly accepted the intrusion, nibbling at his lips before letting her own tongue join in the twisting, turning dance of exploration. She accepted his kisses, his touches and answered them with a passionate hunger.

They parted for the second time, standing up, but moving only a fraction of an inch apart, their breaths coming in sharp, ragged gasps.

"If we don't stop now..." Gavin didn't need to finish his thought.

"I know," Madeline said. Her face was flushed and every fiber of her being sizzled with long suppressed passion and desire.

"Do you want me to leave?"

Madeline could only shake her head.

Gavin's breathing was shallow and rapid. He hesitated only a moment before pulling her against him, lifting one hand to stroke her breast. Her nipple grew rigid in response to his touch.

Madeline pushed into Gavin then moved back just far enough to cup her fingers around his throbbing need. When she gave it a suggestive squeeze, a primitive groan escaped from someplace deep in Gavin's chest.

"What are you doing to me, babe?" he asked, the guttural notes of his voice punctuating the air around them.

"Nothing you aren't doing to me," Madeline responded, her eyes issuing a clear invitation.

Madeline shrugged out of her blouse and dropped it on the floor. She pulled off her bra and tossed it on top of the blouse. Her jeans and panties came off in one swift motion and landed somewhere on the floor.

Gavin gasped when he saw Madeline standing there, naked. He ripped off his t-shirt. He fumbled a second or two with the button of his jeans before jerking them off, not caring where they fell.

"I almost forgot." Gavin's voice was harsh. "We're undressed, but somebody needs to get dressed."

Madeline stretched out on the couch and opened her arms to Gavin. She shuddered when Gavin, seeking relief from the ache in his loins, entered her completely with the first thrust. She wrapped her legs around Gavin's back, arching to meet his continued thrusts into the secret place of her that demanded his entrance.

Later, spent, they sat on the couch, wrapped in content and in each other's arms. Finally, Gavin broke the silence.

"I don't really want to, but I'd better go home." He gently pulled her to her feet beside him and handed her the clothing she had thrown to the floor. What should have been an awkward moment of redressing seemed very natural and easy. "

I'll call you tomorrow, Madeline." He kissed her tenderly and left, after glancing back towards her one more time.

Madeline sunk down on the couch, wondering what to do about Gavin now. After tonight's ardent union, it was impossible not to. She savored every moment of this evening, from his arrival at her front door to their explosive lovemaking. The memory of their first kiss, although delightful, faded away like last night's stars.

Okay, she decided, maybe a romantic gesture and romance do have something in common. Getting up to go to bed, her thoughts in total jumble, she attempted to sort them out. *I've had sex before, but it had never felt like this. That's what those times had been—just sex. The guys moved on and so did I, which was fine. Gavin and I just met; we don't have any kind of relationship. He will probably move on, too. Had tonight been the start of romance or just raw sex?* Madeline didn't have the answer to that.

****

Gavin hadn't wanted to leave as abruptly as he had, but he was running scared. He wanted to spend the night with Madeline, wrapping her in his arms and in his love. When that "l" word popped into his head, Gavin knew he was in trouble. There would be no spending the night with Madeline Spencer on this or any other night.

Yeah, right. Who am I kidding? I'm only denying the inevitable if I think I won't be spending the night with Madeline. And soon.

Chapter Twelve

"Joe, is it okay if I take lunch at one today?" Madeline asked, slipping into her lab coat.

He mentally reviewed the day's schedule for a second before answering. "Sure thing. Big plans with Gavin?"

"Actually, no," Madeline said. "It's kind of a secret, Joe. I'll tell you all about when I come back this afternoon." Madeline finished adjusting her lab coat and the supplies in the pocket. "Speaking of big plans, I hear you're going out with Kelly on Friday. I think that's awesome, Joe."

"Thanks, Maddy." Joe was not forthcoming about these plans and Madeline didn't pursue the matter.

She walked away, shaking her head. That macho male reticence again. Oh well, she would get the details from Kelly when she got back from the DMV.

A few minutes before one o'clock, Madeline left the hospital and made her way to the DMV office a mile away. She was really starting to appreciate how close everything was in Heron's Cove, and how little traffic there was compared to Seattle. Madeline figured it would make riding again that much easier for her.

Once inside, she sat down at the computer monitor and twenty minutes later she stood at the counter.

"Congratulations. A perfect score." The clerk looked at her over his half glasses as though not believing anyone was capable of attaining a perfect score without cheating.

Madeline couldn't tell if he was impressed, or just spouting words, but she didn't care. After all these years, she once again had a learner's permit to ride a motorcycle.

"You understand that with a learner's permit you can't ride at night, across state lines, carry passengers or ride on the freeway, right?" The clerk's monotone voice was as listless as the air in the little office. He looked at

Madeline, waiting for her to indicate understanding of his instructions.

"Yes, I understand." Madeline had no desire to do any of the things the officer had just mentioned.

When she got back to work, Madeline handed Kelly her driver's license.

Kelly glanced at the license and then turned a blank look on Madeline. "Why did just give me your license?"

"Look." Madeline pointed to the letter indicating she now had a learner's permit to ride motorcycles. "I have a learner's permit. That means I can practice riding motorcycles."

"That's great, Madeline." There was no enthusiasm in Kelly's voice.

The minute she came back from taking the test Madeline had noticed Kelly wasn't her usual ebullient self. She turned her focus to her assistant.

"Is something bothering you, Kelly?"

"Can I talk to you for a minute?"

"Sure, Kelly. Let's go to my office."

Kelly followed Madeline, but remained standing in the doorway.

"What's up?" Madeline asked, sitting on the edge of her desk.

"Well, I was wondering...um...if you and Gavin would go out with us on Friday." Kelly shifted from one foot to the other. "I could ask Joe if you say yes. I know Joe will agree."

"Kelly, come in and sit down. You're making me nervous." Madeline hoped her warm smile would put the younger woman at ease.

Kelly sat in a chair across from Madeline's desk and began picking imaginary lint from her pant leg.

"Why do you want Gavin and me to go out to dinner with you and Joe?"

"I'm nervous about Friday, Madeline." Kelly looked up from her lint picking. "Joe's my boss." Alarm built in her voice.

"I certainly don't have a problem with you and Joe going out. Joe obviously doesn't have a problem, or he wouldn't have asked you. And, Kelly, keep this in mind.

Joe wants *you* to have dinner with him. He didn't ask Gavin and me. So go out Friday and have fun."

Kelly smiled then, the first time since she had entered Madeline's office. "Thanks, Madeline. It really is cool about your permit. Are you going out with Gavin Friday?"

"No," Madeline said. "At least I don't think we're going anyplace, but we're going to a kid's birthday party on Saturday afternoon."

After Kelly left her office, Madeline called Gavin and got his voicemail.

"Hi, Gavin. Call me when you get a chance. I've got good news." She hung up, silently cursing both voicemail and answering machines. She wanted to share her news with Gavin, not some faceless, soul-free piece of technology.

Gavin returned Madeline's call at four-thirty that afternoon.

"Hi. What's your good news?" he asked.

"I went out this afternoon and took my written test."

Gavin was silent until the import of Madeline's words struck him and he started babbling. "You mean? I had no idea. How did you do?"

Madeline laughed. "Yes, my written test to get my learner's permit. I didn't tell anybody what I had planned. I would've shared the results no matter what, but I wanted to wait until the test was over. By the way, I aced it."

"That's the best news I've heard all day. Congratulations, babe. I knew you could do it once you made up your mind."

"Gavin? There's something else," Madeline said.

"What is it?"

"Well, I've decided...that is...um...I don't want to wait for my mom to get here. If you don't have to work or anything tonight or tomorrow, I want to try riding your bike. If the offer is still good."

"I take it back. No, no, not the offer. Your asking to ride my bike is even better news than your permit. We can't do it tonight, though. I've got two jobs. But my calendar is clear for tomorrow. I'll pick you up after work."

Madeline's sigh of relief was audible. "Joe's is the perfect place to practice. He's out on a call right now, but he will be thrilled and probably want to be there."

"You know, with your experience, riding my bike won't be that much different than riding a smaller one. You'll be able to take your road test in no time. Maybe even before your mother gets here."

"Whoa," Madeline chuckled at his enthusiasm. "One step, and a small one, too, at a time."

"Whether you realize it or not, you've taken some mighty big steps in a very short time. I can't wait until tomorrow afternoon."

"Me, either," Madeline said.

When she was off the phone Madeline questioned whether she really was looking forward to the next afternoon. *If I'm shaking this hard tomorrow, I won't be able to ride, that's for sure.*

Madeline finally got a chance to talk to Joe just before they left work.

"Joe, I want to talk to you about Friday." When it looked like he might protest, Madeline plunged forward. "I'm glad you're going out with Kelly."

Joe looked at Madeline for a couple of beats. "You know," he said, "I kinda worried about it. Inter-office dating and all that. Impropriety. Favoritism. How it would look and everything."

"How it would look to whom?" Madeline asked.

"Our clients. You."

"Me?" The one word response squeaked out of Madeline's mouth. "I've already told you how I feel about it. Besides, it's nobody's business except yours and Kelly's. Joe, you've been so good to me, so concerned and supportive and I love you for it. Now I think it's your turn to grab some happiness for yourself."

****

Gavin picked Madeline up at five thirty on Thursday and they rode to Joe's house. Joe had been thrilled to hear about Madeline's riding practice and had agreed to stay in the house and not watch. "But we are definitely celebrating afterwards," he had told her.

"The first thing I want you to do is just sit on the bike," Gavin said. "Make sure your feet can touch the ground. Then stand up and straddle the bike. Your feet should touch the ground when you straddle the bike, too. Try it."

Madeline did this as the good, and bad, memories of her riding years swept over her. Then she looked straight ahead and saw Scott standing there, watching her and grinning. She got off the bike and shook. The day had been glorious and the temperature was still in the seventies at six-thirty, but Madeline shuddered as though trying to ward off a sudden chill. The leather jacket she wore was no help.

"I can't do this, Gavin," she said. "It's too hard." She turned her back on the motorcycle and started to walk away.

"You aren't giving up without at least trying," Gavin said.

"I did try and I can't do it." Madeline tried to walk past Gavin and head for the house.

"Can't do it, or don't want to do it?" Gavin blocked her path to Joe's front door. "We'll take as much time as you need, Madeline, but I won't let you just quit. You've come too far to do that. Scott would want you to ride again." Gavin waited.

They spurred something deep inside Madeline. She looked into Gavin's eyes and saw only pride and encouragement etched on his face.

"Okay, I'll try again," Madeline said, hoping practice was over for the day. "For Scott."

"Madeline, it's great you want to do this for your brother, but it's even more important you do it for yourself."

"I know, Gavin." Madeline made no move toward the motorcycle.

She soon found out practice wasn't over just yet.

"Okay," Gavin said, "let's try the sitting and straddling again."

"Good," he said when Madeline did this successfully for the second time. "Do you remember the gears?" he asked.

"First gear down. Neutral. Second, third, fourth and fifth gears up," Madeline said. "On your bike anyway. On some cycles fourth gear is the highest. You shift with your left foot and brake with your right foot."

"And when should you use the front brake?" Gavin asked.

"You should always use both brakes at the same time," Madeline said. "The front brake is safe to use as long as you remember to squeeze it firmly, but gently. No grabbing it. Otherwise you might end up going ass over teakettle."

Gavin laughed when he heard this. "I don't know where that expression came from, but it tells me you have a clear understanding of the front brake's power."

Gavin showed every indication of continuing the lesson. "Okay, good, but you're not done yet. I want you to start the bike and ride in a straight line to where my helmet is on the ground. When you get to the helmet, turn around and ride back to me. Ready?"

"No," Madeline said, but she did as Gavin requested. The first ride down and back was more difficult than she had expected it to be. She couldn't keep the bike from wobbling, she didn't shift smoothly and a couple of times she stalled the bike. When she stopped she could feel the sweat covering her hands inside the gloves, popping out on her face, and running down the rest of her body.

She told Gavin, but he wasn't concerned about any of this. "Do it again," he said, "and this time, get rid of the wobble."

By the time Gavin decided they were nearly through for the day, Madeline had made a dozen trips down and back. He also had her practice some more advanced riding maneuvers like emergency stops and swerving. Not once did she come close to dropping the motorcycle.

"One more thing," Gavin said. "Ride down the road roughly a mile, turn around and come back here."

"By myself?"

"Yup. By yourself. You're not ready to carry passengers yet." Gavin grinned from ear to ear.

"I can't believe I did all this today," Madeline said. "I didn't want to do any of it at first, but when I sat on your bike, I went immediately back to that time in my life when I rode every day."

"Your experience with bikes really shows, Madeline. Sure, you had a few rough moments to start, but now you ride like you've never been away from a bike."

Madeline could feel Gavin watching her as she set off down the road. She could also feel tension, but at the same time she felt exhilaration coursing through her body. *Why did I ever quit riding?* Madeline was tense, but it was tension born of excitement.

"Madeline, I am so proud of you." Gavin enfolded her in a huge hug when she retuned from her solo ride. "Tomorrow afternoon I'll borrow Denny's bike and we'll go for a ride."

"I'll ride his bike, right?" Madeline remembered Dennis's motorcycle was smaller than Gavin's. A Sportster 1200, like her mother's.

"Nope. You'll ride mine."

"You must be kidding," Madeline said. "I'm not even close to being ready."

"You're ready," Gavin said as they walked up to the house.

Madeline noticed Joe peeking out the window just once, in time to see her attempt to walk up the path to his front door. Now that practice was over, Madeline ran to Joe when he stepped out on his porch and hugged him in celebration of her riding.

At home that night, Madeline examined the events of the day. Work was going well, but she had expected that. Her personal life seemed fraught with confusion and she wondered if she was falling in love with Gavin. Maybe. She certainly didn't want to. At least she didn't think she did. Love was one complication she definitely did not need in her life at this point.

For the first time since telling her parents she didn't care what happened to her motorcycle after the accident, Madeline found herself wondering who was riding it now and wishing she still had it. She had worked hard to earn the money to buy her Sportster 883, refusing financial help from her mom and dad. She recalled the conversation she had with them just before she bought her bike.

"You've always taught Scott and me that we had to work for things we wanted, that we shouldn't expect them to be handed to us just because we have money."

Madeline knew it wouldn't be too much longer before she bought another motorcycle, but she still missed her first one.

"Okay, here's the deal," Gavin said before they started their ride the next afternoon. "I'm the leader for the first half of the ride. That means you go where I do. I won't let you quit unless there is a very good reason."

Madeline was glad her learner's permit wouldn't let her ride across state lines otherwise Gavin would head for the bridge that spanned the Columbia River, connecting Washington and Oregon. It was a gorgeous span, over four miles long with a long upgrade close to the Oregon side and a couple of pretty tight turns. Madeline just didn't feel ready to face that.

Gavin made sure that first ride was mostly on straight roads and away from heavy traffic. When they encountered curves, Madeline took them with relative ease.

At the halfway point, Gavin pulled into the parking lot of a small café.

"That wasn't so bad, was it?" he asked as they went inside.

"It was awesome," Madeline said with a conviction that surprised her.

"When you get your endorsement, we'll go on a poker run. There's one coming up in a couple of weeks," Gavin said.

"We used to go on those all the time," Madeline said. "I never had any luck with the poker hands, but the riding was the best part anyway.

"Did you stop to think that I might not have my endorsement back by the time of that run?"

"Nope." Gavin's one word answer brimmed with confidence.

"What's your background with motorcycles?" Madeline asked when they had given their orders to the waitress.

"I grew up around bikes just like you did," Gavin

said. "Wasn't into racing like you and Scott but I rode for fun, every chance I got. Went on a lot of poker runs and did my share of winning. Also learned to fix anything that could go wrong on a bike. I've got my dad to thank for that."

"So your parents rode like mine did?" Madeline asked.

"Mom only ever rode as a passenger, and I think she did that just to please my dad. She lost her desire to ride and dad did, too, eventually." Gavin grinned. "By then it was too late for me to give it up as I was already hooked."

After eating sandwiches and drinking two cups of coffee each, Gavin and Madeline were ready to finish the ride.

"All right, Madeline. Take us back to Denny's house."

****

As he rode behind her back to Denny's house, Gavin found he was experiencing bewilderment over the turns in his personal life. He wasn't ready to admit he was falling in love with Madeline, but he realized things could never be the same for him again, with or without her. Once they had made love, Gavin knew he had taken an irreversible step. He was willing to walk whatever road Madeline Spencer might lead him on. Even if that road was a dead-end.

Chapter Thirteen

In a parking lot across the street from Murphy's Pizza, a late model, dark green sedan blended in with the other cars and SUVs. The woman behind the wheel of that car watched for the little boy to show up. It was the kid's birthday. He'd told her about the party, practically invited her. *If things go my way, I'll be able to grab him today which will only work if that goon isn't around.* Growing tired of watching the entrance, the woman let her attention wander. It was hot, probably in the nineties, although she hadn't heard or seen the temperature. The windows of her car were rolled down and the warm, sticky air was fogging her concentration. The rumble of a motorcycle engine sharpened the woman's focus once more. A man and a small child were on the cycle and it pulled into Murphy's parking lot. Once the helmets were off, she didn't recognize the man, but she recognized the child immediately. It was the little boy who had been holding the bird. The one she was sent to gather information about. *Too bad that goon took my camera. Well, he won't get that same chance today.* She raised the replacement disposable camera to her eye. *This is really sweet.*

****

The guest list for Cody's party included kids from his daycare and their parents, people Gavin and Dennis worked with at the power company and, of course, Gavin and Madeline. He had picked Madeline up at twelve-thirty and they arrived at Murphy's fifteen minutes later.

"Madeline, I meant it when I said you really didn't have to buy Cody anything," Gavin said. "It's enough for him that you're here."

"I know, but I couldn't resist. I went shopping Monday after work and, I found a shark storybook and a

T-shirt with a picture that almost matches the shark in the book." Madeline added her package to the pile of gifts brought by the other guests.

Murphy's Pizza was one of the largest buildings in Heron's Cove. There was ample room for Cody's birthday party to be semi-private without infringing on patrons not connected to his celebration. The section where the party was to be held had been decorated with red, yellow, blue and orange balloons along with paper streamers. The menu of the day would include pizza, hamburgers and individual ice cream cakes for dessert.

Cody spotted Gavin and Madeline almost as soon as they walked in. He left the game he was playing with friends and rushed over to them.

"Hi, Uncle Gavin. Hi, Madeline. I already told Dad like he said to."

"Told him what, Cody?" Gavin asked.

"That lady's here," Cody said.

Sometimes getting information from Cody was difficult to say the least. His answers came one at a time and Gavin reminded himself to be patient.

"What lady?" he asked.

"The one who was at my house looking at Mako," Cody said.

"She's here, inside?" Gavin quickly checked the interior of Murphy's, but he saw no one matching his recollection of the woman in question.

"No," Cody said. "Outside, in the parking lot. In that green car."

Gavin didn't wait to hear anything else. He grabbed Dennis and together they ran out of Murphy's.

"Cody just told me that lady was outside, in the same green car," Gavin said.

"Yeah, he told me, too."

"Did you see anything?" Gavin asked.

"Not really. I was just in time to see a green car pulling out of the parking lot. Wasn't close enough to get a plate number."

Gavin and Dennis scanned the parking lot and the immediate area around Murphy's. There were no green vehicles of any kind in the parking lot or parked on the street nearby.

"No sign of the car," he told Madeline when he and Dennis came back a few minutes later.

"Madeline, guess what, guess what?" Cody gave them no chance to offer birthday greetings, or ask any more questions about the mystery lady, once Gavin was back inside.

"Whoa, little buddy," Gavin said. "Slow down."

Cody took a breath. "Guess what I got for my birthday from Dad and Uncle Gavin?"

"What?" Madeline asked.

"A motorcycle," Cody said. "It's a little one and I can't ride it on the road. Do you wanna go see it? I got grounded because I talked to that lady. Dad said I couldn't ride for a week. He let me ride with him today 'cause it's my birthday."

At this news Madeline went pale and Gavin wondered if she might launch right into a panic attack. She smiled weakly at Cody. "That's great, Cody," she said, forcing an enthusiasm in her voice she didn't look like she felt.

"You bet we want to see it," Gavin said. "But you can't leave your guests. That would be rude. How about if we go see it after the party?"

"Okay," Cody said, and he ran back to his friends.

"Madeline, are you okay?" Gavin looked at her with concern.

"I'm okay. Just a slight headache."

Gavin chuckled. "I know what you mean. This kind of noise isn't something I'm used to, either."

****

Indeed, the noise level inside Murphy's was near deafening with ten kids from ages three to twelve in attendance for Cody's party. But it wasn't the commotion of celebrating children and their parents that triggered Madeline's distress, and it wasn't even the noise of the whistling video games. It was the sound of tires squealing. Metal ripping from metal. Sirens. So many sirens.

The minute she heard about Cody's punishment, she felt herself hurled back to that day when Scott had been grounded because of his slipping grade in English. Her little brother had been seventeen years old and Madeline had given in to his pleading to go for a ride.

Madeline knew she should make an effort to enjoy Cody's party, for his sake and for Gavin's, but she finally realized it wouldn't be possible. She couldn't shut out the sound of the sirens. She had to get away.

"Madeline?" Gavin's question pulled her back to the present.

"I'm sorry," she said. "Guess I wandered for a minute. Gavin, would you take me home?"

"Now? Cody's ready to open his presents."

"Please?" Madeline offered no explanation for her request.

He looked at her for a split second and then said, "Sure. I'll just go tell Denny we're leaving."

"I'll meet you by the bike." Madeline hurried out of Murphy's.

Gavin didn't say anything until they got back to Madeline's house.

"What happened back there?" he asked, making no move to sit down.

Madeline looked at him and then glanced at the couch. Was it only last Tuesday they had made love there? Now Gavin looked like someone who had never been in her house before, like someone she didn't know.

"I told you. I don't feel well." She sat stiffly in her old gray recliner.

Gavin felt his annoyance gathering force, threatening to dislodge all common sense. He felt no desire to curb it.

"You seemed fine until Cody told you he'd been grounded for talking to a stranger."

Madeline knew she had to respond. Taking a deep breath, she gave an explanation she hoped Gavin would understand.

"When Cody told me he couldn't ride for a week, I didn't see him; I saw Scott." Her words rushed out like a torrent of flood water.

"That's it, isn't it? It's all about you and Scott. Is Scott the only person who matters in your life?"

Madeline, tears already trickling down her cheeks,

didn't say anything for a few beats of time. "That's not fair. How can you ask me that? You don't know what you're talking about." She took a big gulp of air. "I was there; I saw him die. You didn't. That's not something you get over easily." Her tears flowed freely now.

Gavin finally sat down, on the very edge of the couch. "Apparently not. It's only been, what, twelve years?" Scorn dripped from his words. "Here's a newsflash for you, Madeline Spencer. Other people have had their hearts broken, too, and somehow they learn to move on. Pushing Cody and me away won't bring your brother back or help you get on with your life.

Gavin continued while Madeline forced herself to listen. It was time and she owed Gavin that much. "I know what it feels like to lose someone, too. Maybe you'll remember me telling you this. I fought in a war. So, yeah, I saw people die, too. When I said Denny saved my life, I didn't tell you the whole story. Oh, that part was true. If it hadn't been for Denny I wouldn't be here now. Just before that grenade landed by me, though, I lost a buddy. Steve. I tried to talk him into staying with us. Told him the medics were almost there. It didn't work. He died right there. In my arms.

Madeline closed her eyes to attempt to hold back images. She made herself open her eyes to focus on Gavin and stay with him in this story.

"When I came home, I didn't care about anything so I drank a lot. That got me arrested once for disorderly conduct." Gavin had been looking all around the room until now when he focused directly in her eyes. "Lucky for me, I had friends who helped me straighten myself out. Madeline, you have people around you who can help you, too. Your mom. Joe. I would willingly be in your corner. But we can't do it all; you have to meet us at least part way."

Madeline's words jerked out of her mouth. "Scott was grounded, too, because his grade in English was falling. If I hadn't given in to him and had made him stay home, he would still be alive."

"Maybe he would, maybe he wouldn't. There are no guarantees in life."

Silence descended in Madeline's living room until the phone rang and the answering machine picked up.

"Hi, Madeline. It's Kelly. You're probably still at the party or out riding. Anyway, give me a call when you get home. Bye." Her upbeat voice sounded completely out of place in Madeline's living room.

Madeline looked down at her hands. She knew Gavin watched her, waiting for some response, even if it might be an outburst.

When Madeline didn't say anything, Gavin rose from his seat on the couch. "I'm going back to Cody's party. After all, it is *his* day. Maybe you'll at least think about what I've said."

"Gavin, wait. Don't go. We can talk about this."

"No, Madeline. When you decide to move past your brother's death and stop seeing Cody as Scott's reincarnation, we might have something to talk about." Gavin walked out, slamming the door behind him.

Then, Madeline collapsed in her recliner and cried until there wasn't a tear drop left in her body, falling into a fitful sleep. She didn't know how long she slept in the chair and she didn't care, but when she woke up she was so stiff she had a difficult time moving.

She picked up the phone to call Joe, but quickly decided against it. Maybe he wouldn't be as brutal as Gavin had just been, but she knew Joe would say many of the same things. Right now she didn't want to hear any more of the truth. She wanted someone to indulge her feelings.

Reluctantly Madeline reached for the phone again. This time she punched in her mother's number. Sylvia Spencer answered in her customary cheerful voice.

"Hello, Mom," Madeline said in return. "I know you're tired from your trip, but..."

"Madeline Marie, you've been crying, haven't you." Sylvia's statement came without preamble. "Is it the nightmares again?"

"No, it isn't. I haven't had any of those since I moved down here."

"Well, something's going on that made you cry. Talk to me, Madeline."

"Mom, I think I ruined a legitimate chance to fall in love again."

"That would be Gavin Marshall, right?"

"Yes, Mom," Madeline said.

"I will be in Heron's Cove before noon tomorrow," Sylvia told her daughter. "This is a matter that requires face to face conversation."

"Mom, I do have some good news, too, although it probably doesn't matter so much now."

"What is it?"

"If I tell you everything over the phone, we won't have anything to talk about when you get here." Madeline laughed for the first time that day.

****

Gavin went back to the birthday party, but the festive mood was ruined for him. Even Cody's continued excitement had little effect on him.

"Uncle Gavin, do you wanna play this cool basketball game?"

"Maybe later, Cody. I just want to rest for awhile."

"Is Madeline sick?" Cody asked. Dennis had told him Gavin was taking her back home.

"She had a headache, little buddy," Gavin said. "She'll be fine."

"Okay," Cody said and he left to rejoin his friends.

Dennis noticed the change in his friend's attitude.

"Hey, man, is everything okay?" he asked after Cody left Gavin to go back to the play area of Murphy's.

"I don't think it is," Gavin said. He and Dennis found a spot away from the party, which was in its wind-down stage anyway.

"What happened when you took Madeline home? You said she wasn't feeling well. I wondered if you were even coming back."

Gavin waited for some customers to walk by before he said anything.

"I told you her brother was killed in a motorcycle accident, right?" Gavin asked.

Dennis nodded.

"Madeline was there, too. She saw the whole thing. When Cody said he'd been grounded, well, it all fell apart for her. She didn't see Cody at that point; she saw her brother on the day he got killed. He had been grounded, too, and Madeline was supposed to make him stay home. She says Cody looks like Scott did at that age."

"Man, that's wicked," Dennis said.

"Yeah, it is. But it's been a dozen years since the accident. Sometimes it seems like Madeline hasn't made any progress in getting over it."

"Are you in love with her?" Dennis asked.

"Cut right to the chase, don't you?" Gavin asked, his features twisting in a grin. "I don't know anymore. I thought I might be, but until she settles with her past, there's no hope for us. Is this the dead-end road you warned me about?" Gavin attempted to put a light touch in his words, but failed.

"Just didn't want to see you get hurt, that's all." Dennis offered some advice. "Sounds like Madeline has survivor's guilt. She's probably wondering why her brother died instead of her. You know, blaming herself somehow for being alive. If I were you, I'd talk to her after she's had a few days to settle down."

"I don't know. I'll think about it. I really unloaded on her. She probably won't have anything to do with me now." Privately Gavin didn't think Dennis's suggestion would do any good at all.

When he got home Gavin said out loud the words he wanted to tell Madeline. "I'm sorry. I had no right to be so hard on you this afternoon. You were right; we can talk about this. We can take all the time you need." He reached for the phone and quickly abandoned his plan to call Madeline. "Hell, she'd probably just let her damn machine take the call when she heard it was me."

With a last look at the phone, Gavin did something he hadn't done since he returned from the war all those years ago. He drank himself into oblivion and passed out on his couch.

****

Across town, the woman parked her dark green sedan and walked into the photography shop, the disposable camera in her hand.

"May I help you?" the clerk asked.

114

"I'm really in a hurry. How soon can I get this film developed?"

The young girl consulted the clock on the wall. It was three thirty. "We can have it ready by four thirty."

"Perfect," the woman said. "I'll be back in an hour."

She hurried out of the shop to her car. Before she started the engine, she flipped open her cell phone and punched in the number for Cody's mother.

"Hello."

"Paula? It's me."

"You got Cody with you, right?"

"Uh, no, Paula, I don't. But I got pictures."

The silence between Seattle and Heron's Cove at that precise moment was louder than the previous conversation.

"You failed to even get pictures last time. Now I want you to get Cody. He's my kid and he belongs with me. Don't come back until you have him. Got it?"

"Yeah, I got it," the woman said, but the line had already gone dead.

She snapped her phone shut and tossed it on the passenger seat.

I've got an hour to get through while I wait for the film. Maybe I'll get lucky and I won't need the pictures.

She navigated her car down the street where Cody and his dad lived, wondering if they would recognize the nondescript green sedan. That goon would, she knew. Well, she would just take her chances. *There must be hundreds of these plain, green cars around here.* Figuring Cody and his dad were probably still at Murphy's after she drove by the house the first time, she made two more passes and then gave up when she detected no signs of activity.

Damn. Now I'll have to spend at least one night in a motel. Doesn't Paula think I have my own life to live? If only the kid had been outside like he was the first time. We'd be on our way back to Seattle and I would be out of Paula's grasp.

Chapter Fourteen

Gavin felt wretched when he woke up at almost noon after his self-imposed night on the couch. His head pounded like drum practice in a beginner's band. The living room threatened to spin out of control. The sun streaming in through his windows did nothing to make Gavin feel better. Little did he know how much more punishment Sunday had in store for him. The sudden shriek of the phone was a precise, and cruel, reminder of what he had done the night before. Holding his head and groaning, he reached out a hand, grappling for the receiver, knocking it to the floor before he actually managed to answer it.

"H'lo." The effort required to force out that little grunt increased the intensity of the throbbing in his head.

"Gavin? This is Mrs. Stewart. You were supposed to mow my lawn today at eleven o'clock. It's twelve o'clock now. You've never missed a scheduled job at my house before. Is everything okay?"

"I'm sorry," Gavin said, making an attempt to speak clearly. "I just woke up and I think I've got the flu. Can I call you back later?"

"Of course you can, dear. Do you want me to bring you some soup?"

"No thanks," Gavin said.

"If you're sure. I hope you feel better soon."

Gavin struggled to his feet after she hung up and shuffled to the bathroom, now holding his head in both hands. The thought of eating anything, even soup, started an ominous rumbling in Gavin's belly. *A couple aspirin. That's what I need.* He swallowed the aspirin with a gulp of water but it wasn't long before he knew the little, white pills weren't what he needed, at least not this soon.

Reaching the toilet just in time, he sank to his knees

and puked until only dry heaves remained. When the turmoil in his guts subsided, Gavin stumbled to his bedroom and fell across the bed, clad in the same jeans and t-shirt he'd worn the night before.

Gavin woke up that evening at six, feeling only slightly better. His headache was gone, but his stomach still felt dicey, like it would reject anything sent down, so he decided against anything to eat. Figuring a shower was called for, he headed once again for the bathroom.

Freshly showered and wearing a pair of clean jeans, Gavin recalled the previous night with more clarity than he cared to and he remembered Mrs. Stewart calling earlier.

"Shit," he said out loud. "That's the first time I've ever blown a job off." Gavin figured Mrs. Stewart would know something was up if he called her back this soon. *Nobody recovers from the flu that fast.*

His thoughts turned to Madeline. Wasn't her mother supposed to be here soon? *I was supposed to meet her, but I guess that's off now after how I talked to Madeline yesterday.*

Gavin hadn't felt this indecisive about anything in long time. He reminded himself of an awkward, unsure, junior-high schooler. The urge to call Madeline was strong even though he had no idea what he would say once she answered the phone, if she answered. He had his hand on the receiver when doubt pushed the urge aside. *I'll wait until tomorrow. Madeline's probably busy with her mother anyway.*

The bad side of him jumped in with a pep talk of its own.

"She was wrong for running out on Cody's party the way she did. Wasn't even sick, just feeling sorry for herself."

The bad side continued to tell Gavin what he wanted to hear. "Gavin, I'd say don't worry about it. Madeline Spencer owes you an apology."

Gavin shook his head. *I guess Madeline and I both have something to be sorry for.*

However, he made no further attempt to call Madeline.

****

Sylvia Spencer pulled into Madeline's driveway just before noon. Madeline heard the distinctive growl of a Harley engine and wondered if it might be Gavin. Even though she still carried some hurt feelings from the dressing down Gavin had given her yesterday, she hoped it would be him. She remembered enough about motorcycles, though, to recognize the difference in sound between Gavin's and her mother's bikes.

She hurried outside to welcome her mother and started feeling better the instant she was enfolded in her mother's arms.

"Just like when I was a little girl, huh?" Madeline asked, pulling back slightly from the embrace.

"You'll always be my little girl, Madeline." She released Madeline from the hug. "Mom, you look fantastic."

At five foot six inches Sylvia Spencer stood the same height as her daughter and she was nearly as slender. Her short, white hair bore the flattened look that comes from wearing a helmet, but it fluffed up again the moment Sylvia ran her fingers through it. Sylvia's snapping, brown eyes gave testimony she was fit and ready for any adventure.

"The yard looks fabulous, Madeline. Gavin Marshall is responsible, right?" When Madeline nodded, Sylvia Spencer continued. "Whatever happened, apologize, no matter whose fault it was. You would never put this much care into a yard."

Madeline laughed. She didn't mind her mother's words in the least. It was well known among her family and friends that she had zero interest in mowing or weed-eating.

"Come on, Mom. Let's go inside before you totally deflate my ego. I'll show you the before pictures I took of the house and the yard. You'll really sing Gavin's praises when you see how bad the yard was."

"Okay, but let me grab some stuff from my trailer first."

Sylvia had a small trailer hooked to her motorcycle, and she went over to unload what she needed for her stay at Madeline's. When she was settled in the guest room, she joined Madeline in the kitchen where she was brewing the requisite coffee and pondering what to do about lunch.

As soon as she entered the kitchen, Sylvia's eyes went to the center of the kitchen table, occupied by the crystal vase holding the yellow roses.

"From Gavin?" she asked.

How does Mom know this? She hasn't even seen the card. "Yes, Mom." Madeline plucked the card from the bouquet and handed it to her mother.

Sylvia read the card and looked pointedly at Madeline, but she didn't say a word. She tucked the card back in the flowers and then noticed Madeline's driver's license propped against the vase.

"Madeline, is there a good reason for your license to be on the kitchen table?"

"Well, yes," Madeline said.

Sylvia picked up the license and zeroed in on the letter indicating a learner's permit. "Good for you, Madeline."

"I put it there just this morning as a surprise for you." Madeline headed towards the table to look at the permit she had once again acquired. "I didn't think I could do it, but Gavin pushed me. I actually rode his bike, Mom. Twice. It's a Road King. He doesn't even know me that well but he didn't doubt I could ride again. He wants, or wanted, me to take the road test on his bike, but I think it's too big."

"You should remember this, Madeline. Once you learn how to ride a small bike, riding a bigger one isn't that much different." Madeline remembered hearing similar words from Gavin.

"There was never a doubt in my mind you could do it, Madeline. I don't know why there should have been one in yours. In fact, I don't know why you ever quit riding. But we'll talk about that later," Sylvia noticed the look on her daughter's face.

Madeline picked up her license and put it back in her wallet. "How long can you stay, Mom?"

"As long as I want to. I'm retired, remember? Why do

you ask?"

"The Fourth of July is almost here. Joe wants to have a party. I also really want you to meet my neighbor, Emma Perry, who's from England. I'd take you over to her house now, but she volunteers at the senior center on Sunday afternoon."

"I'll at least stay through the Fourth," Sylvia said, "so there will be plenty of time for me to meet Mrs. Perry. Now...what happened between you and Gavin?"

Madeline knew it was no good stalling and she also knew her mother would settle for nothing but the complete story. She took a deep breath and plunged in.

"Yesterday afternoon we went to a birthday party for the son of Gavin's best friend. I thought I was fine until Cody, he's the little boy, told me he got grounded because he talked to a stranger. I couldn't help but remember Scott had been grounded that day and I was supposed to make him stay home."

"Cody reminded you of Scott?" Sylvia said. "This probably wasn't the first time somebody reminded you of your brother and it won't be the last."

"Yes, Cody reminded me of Scott. Wait 'til you see him, Mom. He looks just like Scott did at that age. Anyway, I asked Gavin to take me home. Said I wasn't feeling well. We left just as Cody was ready to open his presents."

Madeline took a deep breath and studied her hands. "Mom, so many people have told me I'm obsessed with Scott's death and Gavin said basically the same thing when he brought me home."

"Those people were right. You do realize you behaved pretty badly yesterday." Sylvia looked like she had a lecture for her daughter; Madeline was glad her mother held back.

"I do," Madeline said. "But I don't know how to fix it."

"I think you do if you'll just stop and think for a minute."

Madeline was quiet for a couple of beats. She knew what her mother meant because she was thinking the same thing. "You think I should call Gavin, don't you?"

"Yes, I do."

"What would I say?" Madeline chewed on her lower lip as she worried, "Suppose he hangs up?"

Now it was Sylvia's turn to chuckle. "Madeline, you're talking like a teenage girl with a crush on the star football player. Tell Gavin you're sorry for how you acted. Tell him you're ready to talk." Sylvia reached out to her daughter. "Will he hang up? Maybe. But if he does, so what? Don't give up. You have to keep trying until you know beyond a doubt that he doesn't want to talk."

"I think you're right, Mom, but can I wait until after lunch?"

"Just like Joe. Always thinking of your stomach. What are we having?"

"That's easy," Madeline said. "Chinese takeout. But I promise I'll cook dinner tonight." She found the number for the Jade Dragon in the phone book. "Joe actually has the number for the Jade Dragon on speed dial, but I've drawn the line at taking that step."

"For someone who is such a talented chef, Joe certainly enjoys eating out. Speaking of chefs, maybe he missed his calling by going to veterinary school. Maybe he should've attended a culinary school. I don't think it would take much persuasion for Joe to open his own restaurant."

Madeline walked in with their food after it was delivered and began setting things out on the table.

"I just talked to Joe and asked him to dinner," Sylvia said. "I assume that's okay." She looked at Madeline and cocked an eyebrow.

"Oh, Mom, of course it's okay. What time is he coming over?"

"He isn't," Sylvia said. "He has plans with Kelly, but he asked for a rain check."

Between lunch and dinner, Madeline and her mother talked about the trip to England, Madeline's new job and life in general.

At five o'clock, Madeline started dinner. "Mom, it's fried chicken and mashed potatoes for us."

"Sounds good," Sylvia said, getting up to help Madeline.

Madeline and her mother had just finished dinner

when it suddenly dawned on Madeline she had forgotten to call Mr. Evans.

"Oh no!" she said.

"What is it?" her mother asked.

"I just remembered I was supposed to call Mr. Evans, my landlord, by the end of the week. Guess I missed that deadline."

"Why were you supposed to call him?"

"I told him I might be interested in buying this house if he ever decided to sell it," Madeline told her mother. "Just before Gavin came over for dinner on Tuesday night, Mr. Evans called. He said he had decided to sell the house and wanted to give me first chance before he listed it."

"Call Mr. Evans tomorrow, Madeline, and let him know whatever you've decided. Right now there's someone else who's more important for you to call. And yes, I noticed you slipped out of your intention to call Gavin after lunch. I'll go to my room so you'll have privacy." She headed down the hall.

"Mom, I'd rather call from my room."

"Suit yourself. Just make the call." Sylvia reversed direction and came back to the living room. She pulled a book from her purse and settled down to read.

Madeline walked slowly down the hall to her room, thinking she'd rather be heading for the dentist's chair and a root canal. She sat on the edge of her bed; her hand shook so much she could barely lift the phone from its base. She hated answering machines, but now she fervently hoped Gavin's machine would pick up. He answered on the third ring.

"Hello." His voice sounded cold.

"Gavin, it's Madeline. Please don't hang up. You don't have to say anything unless you want to. Just hear me out."

"I'm listening." His tone said he wouldn't make it easy for her.

"I just want you to know I'm sorry for walking out on Cody's party yesterday. He's a little kid and you wouldn't let him be rude by leaving his guests. I'm supposed to be a grownup, but I acted like a selfish brat. I'll talk to Dennis and Cody, too, but I wanted to call you first. I hope you'll feel like talking to me again. Thanks for giving me this chance to try and explain myself." Madeline took a deep breath to silence. "Again, thank you. Bye."

"Madeline, wait. I don't want you to hang up, either. I'm sorry, too. I came down pretty hard on you yesterday. Too hard."

"Now I think I probably deserved it," Madeline said, "but I sure didn't yesterday. I was too busy feeling sorry for myself."

"Do you want me to tell Dennis you're going to call?"

"I'd like nothing better than for someone to make this all better for me, but this is something I need to do myself. Thanks for your offer, though."

"Did your mother make it down?" Gavin asked.

"She did. She insisted I call you tonight."

"Why would she do that?"

"After you left my house, I called her and she knew I was upset about something. I didn't want to tell her why over the phone so she squeezed it out of me today.

"How did that go?" Gavin asked. "I hope you didn't tell her what a total jerk I was."

"Mom empathizes, maybe even sympathizes to some extent. But she is also a great practitioner of tough love. I know she won't let me wallow in self-pity. Never has." Madeline paused as she pictured her mother and their earlier conversation. "I couldn't tell her you were a jerk, Gavin, because you weren't. In fact, I was scared to call you, but I'm glad Mom pushed me."

Madeline stumbled a bit over her words as she started an invitation, "Mom would like to meet you. Would you like to come for dinner tomorrow? Or maybe Tuesday?"

Gavin uttered an unfunny laugh. "I'll have to let you know about the day. I started to call you yesterday, but then I chickened out and did something stupid."

"What happened?" Madeline asked.

"I drank myself into a stupor and passed out on my couch. Boy, did I pay a price for that. Didn't wake up until noon and I was so sick that death by hanging would have been preferable. I had a job scheduled at eleven and completely missed it. That's the only time I've done that.

Anyway, I'll have to reschedule the job."

"I understand," Madeline said. "Gavin?"

"Yes?"

"When you decide what day works for you, I want to go see Cody's motorcycle first. He was so excited about it yesterday."

"Madeline, you know what this means. Are you ready for that?"

"I do know. I'll undoubtedly see Scott, but maybe it's time I move past that as you suggested. It's time I started *making* myself be ready.

Madeline finished her discussion with Gavin and headed out to share her relief with her mother. She smiled as she walked into the living room and found Sylvia curled up on the couch, her book lying on the floor.

"Mom, wake up," Madeline said, shaking her mother's shoulder gently. "It's time to go to bed."

Sylvia sat up, taking a few seconds to get her bearings. "Did you call Gavin?"

"Yes, I did," Madeline said. "We were on the phone for almost two hours."

"Is everything okay?"

"It's not okay yet," Madeline told her, "but I think it will get better."

"At least you talked to each other," Sylvia said. "That has to count for something."

****

Gavin was reluctant to let himself think a relationship with Madeline might be possible. At this point, he wasn't completely sure he wanted one. Even with his own uncertainty, he couldn't stop the surge of hope coursing through his body when he hung up the phone.

He was only too aware of the heat spreading in the lower region of his body and of the increasing hardness constrained by his jeans. *Maybe I should stop wearing clothes. As long as I keep thinking about Madeline it would be a lot more comfortable.*

Chapter Fifteen

"Madeline, you need a cat."

Sylvia and her daughter sat at the kitchen table Monday morning, finishing the last of their breakfast.

Madeline wasn't surprised at her mother's suggestion. Sylvia had three cats, presently being cared for by her neighbor in Seattle. "You haven't even met Gavin yet and you sound almost like him. He thinks I should get a dog. Even offered to build a fence if I wanted one. I wanted to settle into the house and my job before I took on the responsibility of a pet. I think I might be ready now."

"Then let's visit the shelter after we shower and get dressed. We should have time to do that before you have to go to work." All three of Sylvia Spencer's cats had been adopted from a shelter in Seattle.

"Great idea," Madeline said.

Joe had called at eight o'clock the night before and insisted Madeline take the day off to spend time with her mother. Madeline refused. In the end they reached a compromise that would bring Madeline in to work at noon.

Madeline lingered now over her second cup of coffee.

"You called Gavin last night."

"Yes, Mom, I did," Madeline said.

"Is he coming over for dinner?"

"That depends. He has to reschedule a job, and he said he'd let me know about dinner when he got this job taken care of."

Madeline told her mother what Gavin had done.

"Poor Gavin," Sylvia said. "He had quite a hangover I'd imagine."

"Poor Gavin? I expect he did have a hangover, but he did it to himself. I don't feel the least bit sorry for him."

The phone rang then, interrupting further conversation between Madeline and her mother.

"Maddy, I'm sorry to disturb your morning, but I really need you to come in right away. I have to go out on an emergency call and…"

"Say no more, Joe. I'll be in as soon as I can get dressed."

Skipping her shower, Madeline hurried into clothes and arrived at the hospital ten minutes later, at ten o'clock.

****

Kelly, normally calm and cheerful, was stressing out over something when Madeline got to the hospital.

"Let's go in my office," Madeline said.

"Joe hated to call you, but he got a call about a horse that got tangled in some wire." Kelly said as soon as Madeline closed the door to her office. "We have an upset woman in the lobby who is demanding to see Joe and only Joe." Kelly jerked her head in the direction of the waiting area. "I tried to explain about the emergency and that you were a doctor, too, but she wouldn't let up on her insistence on talking to Joe. There are also two people waiting with their cats that were brought in for spay surgery."

"It's all right, Kelly," Madeline said. "I'll talk to the woman and you can set up the operating room for me."

Madeline watched her assistant hurry off to set up for the surgeries. Then she returned to the lobby and talked to the woman waiting to see Joe, easing her concerns.

Joe returned a little after one. Madeline was still in surgery so Joe went in to assist her.

"How did the emergency go?" Madeline looked up at Joe coming in.

"He narrowly escaped tearing a tendon in his leg."

Other small talk was exchanged throughout the surgery until they had the cat settled in recovery.

"Madeline, Gavin called while you were in surgery." Kelly stuck her head in the break room to deliver her message.

"Thanks, Kelly," Madeline said. "Did he leave a

message?"

"Just said that Tuesday was okay for dinner." Kelly went back to the front desk.

Madeline punched in Gavin's cell number and hung up seconds later. She groaned loudly.

"Voice mail?" Joe looked at her, one eyebrow curving up his forehead.

"Sometimes it seems like all we do is play telephone tag," Madeline said.

Madeline was in her office catching up on some paperwork when Kelly told her twenty minutes later that Gavin was on line one.

"Hi, Gavin."

"You sound exhausted. Busy day?"

"Joe insisted I take the day off to spend with my mother, but he had to bring me in when he got an emergency call. We've been going nonstop until now. I take it you got your job rescheduled."

"Yeah, for tonight at five-thirty," Gavin said. "Is the dinner invitation for tomorrow still good?"

"Of course it is," Madeline said. "We'll have dinner at six-thirty, but please come over before that."

"Will do," Gavin said. "What do you want me to bring?"

"Just yourself," Madeline said. "Does Dennis have to work late tonight by any chance?"

"No," Gavin said. "As a matter of fact, he just left the room."

"I'd like to talk to him if he's willing," Madeline said.

"Hold on. I'll go see if I can catch up with him."

Madeline was grateful she had a little time to think about what she would say to Dennis *if* he agreed to talk to her. While she waited, she tried to calm her breathing.

"Yo," Dennis said by way of greeting.

"This is Madeline. I was wondering if I could stop by your house tonight after work. I really need to talk to you."

"Uh...sure...I guess," Dennis said. "Do you know where I live?"

"No, I don't. Sorry," Madeline said.

Dennis gave Madeline directions to his house and

handed the phone back to Gavin.

"Everything all set?" Gavin asked.

"Yes. I'm going over there at five-thirty. I want to apologize to Dennis and Cody. Not to mention, I want to see Cody's motorcycle. He didn't sound too enthused about seeing me. I guess I can't expect a warm welcome, can I?"

"It'll be okay, Madeline, but I still wish I could be there with you," Gavin said.

"I wish you could be, too, but I'll be fine, Gavin."

"Well, I'll call you later to find out how it went."

Joe stopped by Madeline's office just as she ended her phone call.

"Maddy, go home. Take a shower, eat dinner, relax. You deserve it. I'll check on our patients later tonight."

Madeline smiled at her friend. "I plan to do exactly that, Joe, but I have something else to do first." She gave him a brief account of her plans.

"You'll be fine," Joe said. "See you in the morning."

"Eight o'clock sharp."

Madeline arrived at Dennis's house about five minutes after he and Cody got home. Her knees were shaking and she had butterflies in her stomach. *You're doing the right thing.* That voice!

When Cody heard Madeline talking to his dad he came charging down the hall from his room.

"Hi, Madeline. Did you come to see my motorcycle?"

"Yes, I did, Cody." Madeline was relieved to know she meant those words. "But first I need to talk to your dad."

Cody stood there expectantly until Dennis spoke up.

"Why don't you go back to your room for awhile, son?"

"Okay." Cody was off again.

"Would you like to come inside?" Dennis asked.

"Thank you," Madeline said, "but that isn't necessary.

"I want to say I'm sorry for running out on Cody's party and spoiling things for you and Cody."

"I'm still not sure I understand what happened, but I appreciate your apology. You have to know, though, that Cody and I will always be a part of Gavin's life."

"I do know that," Madeline said. "And if I want to…" She broke off, not wanting to finish the sentence with

...be a part of Gavin's life. "Now I think it's time I looked at a certain motorcycle."

Dennis called for his son then and Cody once again came running down the hall. He took Madeline's hand and led her to the garage where his prize possession was parked.

"That is one sweet bike, Cody," Madeline said.

The little boy's chest swelled with pride.

"You know what?" Madeline asked.

Cody shook his head.

"My brother, Scott, got a motorcycle almost like this when he was five. For Christmas." The lump in Madeline's throat was growing smaller in the telling.

"Maybe him and me can ride together," Cody said.

Silence took brief control.

"I don't think so, Cody," Madeline said.

"Why not?" Cody asked.

Madeline wasn't sure if the child had any religious training or beliefs, so she hesitated briefly before giving him an answer. She looked up in time to see Dennis's eyes on her, a look of horror spreading on his face.

"Um, he's in heaven."

"You mean with Jesus?" Cody asked.

"Yes. With Jesus."

Thinking this was probably a good time to change the subject, Madeline moved to the real purpose of her visit. "Cody, I'm sorry I left your birthday party on Saturday and missed watching you open your presents."

"That's okay. Uncle Gavin said you were sick. Are you feeling better?"

"Oh yes. I'm feeling much better, Cody. Thank you for asking."

Just then the phone rang.

"I'll get it, Dad."

Dennis shook his head laughing as he watched Cody disappear into the house. "That kid loves to answer the phone. Can you believe he's trying to convince me he needs a cell phone?"

"I can," Madeline said. "My brother would've convinced my parents to get him one if they had been more popular then."

"I'm sorry. I mean about Cody asking you about your brother," Dennis said.

"My brother died twelve years ago. I think it's time I got used to talking about him and to hearing others talking about him."

Madeline and Dennis chatted for a few more minutes and then Dennis excused himself.

"I'd better go make sure Cody isn't talking to a telemarketer and plunging me into debt. Thanks for stopping, Madeline. We appreciate it."

Madeline drove home then, feeling like she was finally beginning to release her emotional baggage.

True to her word, Sylvia had dinner ready when Madeline got home.

"Mom, you're an angel," she said after her much needed shower.

****

When Dennis went back inside, Cody still had the receiver pressed to his ear, but he wasn't saying anything.

"Give me the phone, Cody."

Cody gave up the phone without protest and remained seated on the couch.

"Hi. Who is this?" Dennis asked.

The voice that answered turned his knees to jelly and he sank down on the couch next to Cody. Dennis realized he couldn't have this conversation in Cody's presence. He put in the DVD of Cody's favorite movie and walked out on the back deck.

"Paula, what the hell do you think you're doing?"

"I called to wish our little boy happy birthday."

"Once again you forgot, Paula. My son turned seven on Saturday so you're two days late. But that's nothing new for you is it?"

"Dennis, that is totally unfair and you know it. I've been sick. For a long time. But I'm well now and I want to see Cody. I'm his mother. It's my right to see him."

Dennis's derisive snort crackled over the line. "You gave up that right when you chose drugs over your son."

"My lawyer says differently, Dennis. She's ready to fight for joint custody. Maybe full."

"It will be a cold day in hell when that happens."

"Cody told me you and Gavin bought him a motorcycle for his birthday, and you've got the balls to call me an unfit parent. My lawyer will be very interested in hearing about that damn bike."

Dennis hung up on his ex-wife. He whirled around when he heard Cody's voice.

"Dad?"

Dennis took his little boy in his arms. "What is it, Cody?"

"Mom said she wants me to live with her in Seattle." Cody lifted his chin in defiance. "I don't want to."

Dennis hugged him close. "Don't worry, son. You won't have to." Dennis hoped he would be able to prevent such a move.

****

"What a delightful young man. Madeline, Gavin is a keeper."

"Mom, you're just saying that because he brought you flowers. Anyway, I can't keep something that isn't mine to begin with."

Sylvia studied her daughter for a long while before she said anything. "How do you feel about him, Madeline?"

"I'm not sure, Mom. After all, we don't know each other very well."

"Well, I can see one thing clearly." Sylvia didn't wait for her daughter to respond. "Gavin is in love with you."

"That's impossible, I just told you we..."

Her mother waved a hand, brushing aside Madeline's protest. "Two people don't always have to have known each other for ages before they fall in love."

"I'm not in love with Gavin. But even if I was, what am I supposed to do about it?"

"That, my darling daughter, is something you have to figure out for yourself."

Madeline thought about her mother's words after she had gone to bed. Higgins, Madeline's newly adopted cat, was curled in a little ball at the foot of the bed. At first Madeline dismissed the idea she might be in love with Gavin. "We've had fun together; he's a nice guy. That's all." Her words, spoken aloud, rang hollow in her ears.

Chapter Sixteen

Gavin had shared some of Dennis's story with Madeline's mother on Tuesday night. Now, a day later, Sylvia pressed her daughter for more details.

"What's the story on Dennis Garrett?"

"I only know what Gavin told me. Dennis's ex-wife is a drug addict, or was. She's supposedly been in rehab for the last two years."

"Has she had any contact with Cody?"

"I don't think so," Madeline said. "Her phone call to Cody on Monday was her first communication with him in at least two years."

"Is Dennis a good father?" Sylvia asked.

"I've only met him a few times, Mom, but I think he's doing the best he can. Cody is in daycare while his dad works, and Gavin watches him sometimes, too."

"Gavin and Dennis are pretty tight, aren't they?" Sylvia asked.

Madeline nodded. "Dennis saved Gavin's life once."

"How did that happen?" Sylvia asked.

"It was during the first Gulf War," Madeline said. "Dennis pushed Gavin out of the way when a grenade landed by Gavin's feet."

"I can see how something like that would bring those two, or anyone for that matter, closer," Sylvia nodded and went to her room. Within a few moments, she came back carrying what Madeline recognized as a photo album.

"I think it's time we looked through this again," Sylvia said, taking a place beside Madeline on the couch. She opened the album and the journey through early family life began.

"There's Scott when he was six years old," Madeline said. "Look at that picture of Scott and you're looking at Cody."

"How do you feel about Cody riding motorcycles?" Sylvia asked.

"I'm still a little edgy," Madeline said, "but it's not my call. Cody isn't my son. He is old enough by law to be a passenger, and Dennis makes sure he wears all the proper gear." She laughed. "So does Gavin."

"It might not be your call whether or not Cody rides, but it could affect your relationship with Gavin."

"Mom, there isn't a relationship between Gavin and me."

"Maybe not yet," Sylvia said, "but there will be."

"Give me time, Mom. I'll adjust. To the Cody part anyway." She turned a couple of pages and there was Scott at his first race.

Madeline could feel her mother watching closely during her perusal of the pictures.

"He was some kind of racer, wasn't he, Mom? Remember when he and I raced each other? Scott beat the stuffing out of me every time except in those two times at that track by our house."

"Yes, he was something all right," Sylvia acknowledged. "That boy lived to be on or around motorcycles. You were always his hero, Madeline."

Madeline sat quietly, considering what her mother had just said.

"I don't know if I ever realized that, Mom."

"Well, it's true, Madeline. He idolized you. It won't hurt your feelings to be reminded he was a much better racer than you were."

This drew a soft chuckle from Madeline. "Lord no, Mom. I was never jealous of Scott's ability. I loved him. I only wanted to keep him safe."

Looking at the old family photos again brought a certain feeling of sadness to Madeline, but at the same time it strengthened the bond with her mother and Scott. Her week had been a busy one so far, so she was content to sit back and rest, looking at the pictures with her mother.

While her mother went to the bathroom, Madeline made a pot of coffee.

"I know it's a little late for coffee, but I wanted some,"

Madeline said when her mother rejoined her in the living room.

"Did you ever call Mr. Evans?" Sylvia asked.

"I did and I told him I wanted to buy the house."

"What did he say?" Sylvia asked.

"Mr. Evans seemed relieved to have the house taken off his hands," Madeline told her mother. "Mom, have you given any thought to moving down here? I'd love to have you closer. You could live here with me."

Her mother hesitated as if carefully choosing her next words. "Actually, Madeline, I have thought about it. There isn't anything holding me in Seattle, but if I did move down here I would eventually want my own place."

"That wouldn't be necessary, Mom."

"Sure it would be. I wouldn't want you cramping my style." Sylvia grinned.

Madeline got up to answer the phone. The caller id told her it was Gavin.

"Hi, Gavin."

"Madeline, I've got a huge favor to ask you."

"Name it." Her answer was swift.

"I told you Cody's mother called, right? And that she's making noise about custody?"

"Yes, you did," Madeline said.

"Well, Denny's pretty upset by all this. I need to talk to him, just the two of us."

"I understand," Madeline said, "but where does the favor come in?"

"Will you watch Cody for a couple hours on Friday? After work?"

"Of course I will," Madeline said, again without hesitation. "And if I have to work late, I'm sure Mom will watch him."

"It would only be for a couple hours, like I said. Cody doesn't need to hear what Dennis and I will be talking about."

"Gavin, it's okay and Cody will be fine here. My mom will love meeting him."

"Meeting who?" Sylvia asked when Madeline was off the phone.

"Scott's look-alike," Madeline said, smiling at her

mother. She filled her in on the plans for Friday night.

On Friday, two days later at five-thirty, Gavin and Dennis dropped Cody off at Madeline's house.

"We'll be back at eight," Gavin said.

Dennis nodded his agreement.

"No problem. We will be just fine here." Madeline assured the guys and sent them on their way before turning to introduce Cody to her mother.

"You were right, Madeline. He does look a lot like Scott did at that age."

"Who's Scott?" Cody asked.

Madeline and her mother exchanged looks over Cody's head, and then Madeline knelt down so she was eye level with him.

"Oh yeah. You told me he was in heaven."

****

Gavin and Dennis's night started with some hastily thrown together sandwiches in Dennis's kitchen.

"I don't know what I'd do if she took Cody away," Dennis said.

"That isn't going to happen, Denny."

"She says she's been clean for a year, but how do I know that? I've only got her word and we know what that's worth."

Gavin searched for a way to reassure his friend. Finding none, he offered a suggestion.

"We can't do anything tonight, that's for sure. Let's go out for one drink before we pick Cody up. Maybe shoot some pool."

Gavin and Dennis headed for Finn's Bar & Grill, which was already bouncing with music and voices when they got there at six-thirty. The minute they walked into Finn's they were hailed by some friends from work. Greetings and high fives were exchanged before Gavin and Dennis found a booth.

Halfway through his second beer Dennis relaxed enough to challenge Gavin to a game of pool.

****

The woman had taken a seat in Finn's that allowed her a nearly unobstructed view of the front door. She was about to scrap her mission when Gavin and Dennis walked in. *I'd recognize Dennis Garrett anywhere.* The picture, now lying wrinkled in her purse, was confirmation.

****

Dennis, well into his third beer, didn't notice a woman shadowing them from booth to pool table and points in between.

Gavin didn't know the woman who seemed to be following them, but he had seen her around town before. It took his beer hazy mind a couple of beats before he realized just where he had seen her. He jumped up from the booth sloshing beer on the table in his haste. She was the same woman who had been talking to Cody in front of his house.

Gavin grabbed a chair and sat on it backwards, facing the woman.

"I don't know what your game is, but you've been following me and my buddy around ever since you came in here. Leave us alone and stay the hell away from his little boy."

The woman blinked slowly, a look of insolence crossing her face. "Don't know what you're talking about. This is a public place. That means I have a right to be here and I don't know anything about any kid."

"Cut the crap, lady," Gavin said. "I caught you talking to the kid a few days ago. Now. I suggest you clear out or I'll..."

"Or you'll what? Hit me? That's probably your style."

Gavin felt the flush creeping up his neck. "If you care about what's good for you, you'll get out. *Now.*" He stood up, enjoying the play of fright and defiance on the woman's face.

Fright apparently won. The woman got up and left Finn's with a parting shot at Gavin. "You haven't seen the last of me," she said.

Gavin went back to the booth he shared with Dennis.

"Hey, buddy, maybe you better slow down on the beer," Gavin said when Dennis ordered his fourth one.

"Gavin, don't be such an ol' lady. Live a little." Dennis's words were slurred and it came out sounding like, 'Live alil.'

"You're right, Denny. I'll have another." Gavin saw no reason to tell Denny about his confrontation with the woman. *He wouldn't remember what I told him anyway.* Gavin ordered a pitcher of beer.

****

When Madeline looked at the clock on her kitchen wall she was shocked to see it was already nine o'clock. She called Dennis's cell; no answer. Next she tried Gavin's cell with the same result.

Cody and her mother had been locked in a fierce battle over the chess board since after dinner. Now Madeline heard Cody's triumphant cry of "Checkmate!"

"Let's play again."

"Nothing doing, you little hustler," Sylvia told Cody. "You already cost me five bucks."

"Mother! You bet a little kid on a game of chess?"

"Makes the game more interesting." Sylvia looked up, a sheepish grin on her face.

"Yeah. Next time we're gonna play poker," Cody said.

"And just what would your dad say about that?" Madeline asked.

"Nothin'. He taught me how to play."

Cody, unaware his dad was late picking him up, lobbied once more for another game of chess. When he got no takers, he went looking for Higgins.

Sylvia yawned and stretched. "I think I'll have a glass of orange juice or something." She headed for the kitchen.

"You let him win didn't you?" Madeline smiled. "That was sweet."

"It might've been sweet if that's what I did, but that little turkey beat me fair and square."

Madeline let it go. "Mom, it's almost nine-thirty and no word from Dennis or Gavin."

"Did you call either one yet?"

"At nine. First Dennis, then Gavin. They both had their cell phones turned off."

"If we haven't heard from them by ten o'clock, try again. Try their home phones in the meantime."

"I already did that," Madeline said. "Left messages at both places."

"It looks like we'll have an overnight guest," Sylvia said.

Madeline and her mother walked back to the living room to find Cody curled up on the couch, his arm around Higgins.

"Hey, sleepyhead," Madeline said, sitting down beside him.

"Is my dad here yet?"

"Not yet, Cody, but he should be soon. Are you getting tired?"

Cody nodded and snuggled deeper into the couch pillows.

When Gavin called at ten, Madeline heard the distinct sounds of a bar in the background—loud music, loud voices and the clank of glass hitting glass.

"Where have you been?" she asked. "Where are you now?"

"Finn's," Gavin said.

"Have you forgotten you were supposed to pick Cody up two hours ago?"

"No. That's why I called. We'll be there in a few minutes."

"I don't think so," Madeline said. "You're drunk. Again."

"Dennis is drunk, Madeline. I'm not. I'll take both of them home."

"You will do no such thing. Do you really think Cody needs to see his dad in that condition? He's almost asleep as it is. He will spend the night here and you or Dennis can pick him up in the morning. If you're sober."

"What makes you think you know what's best for Cody?" Gavin asked.

"I know better than to let him get in a vehicle with a couple of drunks."

"Hey, Cody, are you awake?" Madeline asked, once again taking a seat on the couch.

"Uh, uh," came his sleepy answer.

"I just talked to Gavin," Madeline said. "Your dad had some trouble with his truck. That's why they haven't picked you up yet."

Madeline figured it was better telling Cody this small

lie instead of the raw truth.

"Are they coming pretty soon?" Cody struggled to sit up, thereby dislodging Higgins.

"Not until the morning. You get to spend the night here."

"Okay," Cody said. "Can Higgins sleep with me?"

"Sure," Madeline said.

Cody was asleep before Madeline tucked him in and kissed him goodnight.

"Is Cody settled in?" Sylvia asked when Madeline came back to the living room.

"He's sound asleep," Madeline told her mother.

Madeline fidgeted for a few moments before her mother spoke up. "Madeline, sit down."

Madeline thumped down on her recliner. "I can't believe this."

"Can't believe what?" her mother asked.

"That Gavin and Dennis could be so irresponsible with Cody. Just when I thought Dennis was doing such a good job."

Her mother looked at Madeline for a minute. "Madeline, if they were irresponsible they would've left Cody with just anybody, or worse yet, left him home by himself."

"But they didn't pick him up when they said they would."

"Okay, Madeline, what's really bothering you?"

"I just told you, Mom."

"I'm not buying a word of it."

Madeline heaved a sigh. "When Gavin came here that first day with Cody, I almost lost it.

"Then we went riding twice and I had fun. Oh sure, I was a little scared, but those rides made me remember how much I used to love riding." Madeline lost some of her momentum. "But I can't, or couldn't get past Cody on a motorcycle."

Her mother said nothing, however, waiting for her daughter to continue. Her wait wasn't a long one.

"Gavin thinks I'm obsessed with Scott's death." Madeline continued. "Mom, all the men who were important in my life left me. First Scott, then Dad."

"You can't possibly think Scott and your dad left on purpose."

"Of course I don't," Madeline said. "But they did leave."

"And you believe Gavin is next. Well, here's a news flash for you, Madeline. You aren't the only person who lost Scott in that terrible accident. I can only imagine how devastating it was for you to watch it happen. Your father and I weren't there, but we lost Scott that day, too."

Her mother continued with a softer voice, "For a long time after the accident, we feared we would lose you, too. You shut everyone out. Joe, us, the doctors. Outwardly, you appeared to be getting on with life, but we all knew you were a mess inside."

Sylvia hesitated for just a moment before continuing, "Madeline, you've never been a selfish person, but you are self-centered. Life isn't all about you. You need to acknowledge other people have problems and feelings. If you can't do that, you may very well drive Gavin away and that would be a shame indeed."

Sylvia wrapped Madeline in a comforting hug. "Let's go to bed. I'm tired and I imagine you have a few things to consider."

Chapter Seventeen

Cody was eating breakfast when his dad called Saturday morning. Dennis apologized profusely to Madeline for his actions the night before. Madeline talked for a while before she handed the phone to Cody.

"Maybe next time Cody and I *will* play poker," Sylvia said after he'd gone home with his dad.

"Mom, you should be ashamed of yourself," Madeline said, but she didn't mean it.

"Perhaps I should be, but I'm not." Sylvia loaded the breakfast dishes in the dishwasher. "Your dad taught you and Scott to play poker."

"But we never played for money. Did we?"

"Yes, Madeline, you did. You were a mean poker player. If memory serves correctly, you amassed quite a collection of your dad's and brother's quarters."

"I nearly forgot. Today's your big day," Madeline said. "What time are you leaving?"

Sylvia hesitated a moment. "Oh, my trip with Mrs. Perry. That should be quite an experience. We planned to leave around one. From what I gather, she is a serious poker player. I prefer the slot machines or the craps table."

"Come back wealthy women," Madeline said.

"Are you seeing Gavin this weekend?"

"I don't know, Mom. After last night, I'm not sure if we'll ever talk to each other again."

"Just remember what we talked about last night," Sylvia said. "You need to be willing to give Gavin a fair chance."

With her mother's words of the previous night fresh in her mind, along with these new words, Madeline knew she would welcome Gavin's call. If he called.

A few minutes later the phone rang and Madeline's

mother answered it. Madeline had gone to her bedroom to make her bed, but she heard her mother's voice, cheerful in its conversation. *It's probably Emma Perry or maybe Joe.* Then she heard her mother's footsteps approaching.

"Madeline, phone call. It's Gavin." Sylvia continued down the hall to her room to take care of packing for her trip.

"Good morning, Gavin."

"Madeline, I am so sorry about last night. I wasn't drunk. Well okay, maybe a little drunk. But just so you know, I called a cab to take Denny and me home. He walked back this morning to get his truck. Has he picked Cody up yet? Was Cody any trouble?"

"Yes, Dennis was here a little after nine. But you didn't tell us Cody was a hustler."

"Huh?" Gavin's tone was blank. "Oh, he snookered you into playing poker, I bet."

"Not me. My mother. They played a game of chess. Cody won the game and five bucks."

Gavin roared with laughter. When the laughing subsided, he asked, "Whose idea was the betting?"

"My mother's," Madeline said.

"Listen, Madeline, would you like to go out tonight? Ask your mother, too."

"I'd love to, Gavin, but it would just be the two of us. My mother won't be here because she's going away for a few days with Mrs. Perry."

"Okay, just the two of us then. I'll pick you up at six. Bike or truck?"

"No bike tonight," Madeline said. "I'd like to wear a dress."

"You got it," Gavin said.

****

Madeline was ready when Gavin picked her up that night. She had chosen to wear a pale blue, sleeveless sundress that fell to knee level. *I spend so much time in jeans or pants. It feels wonderful to wear a dress.*

"Good evening, Ms. Spencer," Gavin said, offering his arm.

"Good evening, Mr. Marshall. Ms. Spencer reminds me of my mother so you may call me Dr. Spencer."

They both laughed.

Gavin and Madeline lingered over dinner at the only steakhouse in Heron's Cove.

"How do you feel about taking a walk on the beach?" Gavin asked when they were finally ready to leave.

"That sounds good to me," Madeline said. "This is such a beautiful night."

They found a parking spot a couple of blocks from the beach and hand in hand started their walk. Madeline took off her shoes as soon as her feet touched sand.

"Feet were meant to be bare when they're walking on sand," she said, slipping the straps of her sandals over her wrist.

Gavin removed his shoes, too, tied the laces together, and slung the shoes over his shoulder.

"How did you get interested in landscaping?" Madeline asked.

"It all started with my mother. She was the artistic one, knew exactly what she wanted in her yard. Dad helped with the heavy work she couldn't do and, of course, I was recruited. At first I hated it, but Mom insisted. Dad and I were powerless to resist her.

"Have you ever thought about opening your own business?" Madeline asked.

"A few times," Gavin said, "but I like the security of my real job. If I did landscaping full time it would become a job. Right now it's almost a hobby."

They walked in silence then, enjoying the night and each other.

"Madeline?" Gavin's utterance was a caress.

Their eyes held for mere seconds before Gavin's right hand cupped the back of Madeline's head, his fingers twisting in her hair. He kissed her then, igniting the fire that had been building in her since their phone call earlier in the day.

"Gavin, we can't possibly, not here on the beach." Madeline felt logic slipping away from her and found she didn't care.

His answer fanned the flames burning in Madeline even higher. Gavin deepened his kiss while his left hand moved slowly down, gently cupping her breast.

"You're right," he said, breaking the kiss and taking his hand away from her breast. For just a brief moment before they parted, she could feel the unmistakable pressure of his swelling desire.

Gavin and Madeline finished their planned walk, although their steps were much swifter on their way back to the truck. There was little conversation on the drive back to Madeline's house.

Madeline was confident of Gavin's answer, but when he walked her to the front door she asked anyway.

"Would you like to come in for awhile?"

"I would." Gavin's voice was rough.

Inside, Madeline poured two glasses of wine and she and Gavin settled on the couch. There was no conversation, only a tangible energy flowing between them.

They looked at each other before Gavin gently cupped her face in his hands, and his lips settled lightly on hers.

For a while Madeline let herself be kissed, enjoying the passion spreading through her body. When Gavin would have drawn back, she pulled him to her, entwining her fingers behind his head and returning his kisses with a quiet fervor.

Gavin's hands slipped from her face, one moving to the back of her head, his fingers clutching the glorious mass of her dark hair, long since released from its clasp. His other hand slid down the length of her arm, coming to rest at the indent of her waist.

Madeline's nipples, already extended, threatened to break through the layers of her bra and dress when Gavin's hand, in its journey down her arm, brushed her right breast. She let go a small sigh of pleasure, her hands moving in their own exploration of Gavin's body.

At first she was content slowly stroking his arms, then his chest, but Madeline quickly tired of this. Her fingers reached beneath the material of Gavin's shirt where they danced through the dark mass of hair on his chest. When they tugged at his nipples, Gavin growled at Madeline to stop, but there was no force in his request.

Madeline's hands moved lower, stopping briefly in their journey downward to caress his rock solid belly. His belly wasn't the only part of his body that was hard. When Madeline cupped one hand over his throbbing manhood, a rumble echoed deep in his chest.

"Oh, God, babe. These damn jeans."

Keeping her contact with Gavin's delicious lips and tongue, Madeline struggled to unfasten the button of his jeans. Her touch seemed to drive him to new heights of madness. With each brush of her hands, his hardness begged for release. Frustrated, Madeline stood, pulling Gavin up with her.

Trying to walk at this point was rather difficult for both of them, especially as they tried to keep contact with each other. Finding a semblance of balance, Gavin picked her up and carried her to the bedroom.

Once in the bedroom, Madeline removed Gavin's clothes with tantalizing slowness. The shirt she just pulled over his head, but she took her time removing the restricting jeans. When at last his clothing lay in a heap on the bedroom floor, Gavin moved to take Madeline in arms, but she stopped his attempt.

"Not so fast, big guy," she said. "I want to look at you." Madeline's own tension increased rapidly as she drank in the sight of his broad shoulders and the muscles defining his chest. As if controlled by an unseen force, her eyes settled on the full hard length of Gavin's maleness. When she began moving her hand unhurriedly along the length of his shaft, he snarled in agony.

"My God, what are you doing to me?" His control seemed to be abandoning him when a single love drop escaped from his pulsing member.

Madeline looked up at Gavin, but said nothing. She closed both hands gently around his aching member, kneeling to kiss the very tip of it.

"Madeline, enough" he said, his voice coming out in a cracked whisper. "It's my turn now."

He pulled her to her feet and moved his hands up her arms and behind her back. He slowly undid the zipper of her dress. When Madeline would have helped him remove her bra, Gavin took both her wrists in one of his hands and shook his head. Gavin unhooked her bra and dropped it on the floor. His hands moved swiftly to rid Madeline of her remaining clothing. Gavin lost his breath momentarily as he stood there looking at her beautiful nakedness.

He picked her up and this time laid her gently on the bed, stretching out beside her and getting as close as his erection permitted. He kissed her forehead, her eyelids, her lips. When he lowered his mouth so he could tease the already stiff nipple of her breast, Madeline became acutely aware of how much she wanted Gavin.

While his teeth and tongue continued to play games with the agitated nipple, Gavin moved his hand down Madeline's belly until his fingers found that hard button above the hot, fiery place of her womanhood. He stroked it until Madeline cried out with a passion and desire to match his. When his fingers slipped inside her, she writhed with abandon and the demand for release. Instead of crying out she reached over to grab his erection, straining for release of its own.

"Madeline, I can't wait anymore."

"I can't either, but first, somebody has to get dressed."

"You're right," Gavin said. "I nearly forgot."

There was no need for Gavin to part her legs; they were open to receive him and Gavin entered her with the full length of his desire. The moment he felt Madeline close around him and pull him deep inside, he came close to the point of spilling his love. He pulled out then and the next few thrusts were slower, more purposeful.

Madeline matched each thrust with an arch of her back, her nails biting into the flesh on Gavin's shoulders as she went over the top, falling deliciously into their shared ecstasy.

With one last deep, forceful drive, Gavin poured his love into that warm, moist place of her.

They parted, content in their mutual satisfaction and closeness.

Sunday morning, Madeline stretched in her sleep, moving over to snuggle against Gavin's back. She woke up abruptly when her arm fell on the cold sheet. Gavin was no longer in bed, but his scent filled the pillow. Madeline burrowed into it.

Sleep evaded her, however, and she got up, stuffing her feet into slippers and shrugging into a bathrobe. It was at that moment she noticed the aroma of bacon frying.

"Gavin?" Madeline picked up her pace to the kitchen.

"In here, babe," he said. "You made breakfast for me once and I'm returning the favor. Bacon and cheese omelettes with toast."

"Don't you have a job today?" Madeline still bore the last traces of sleep and she couldn't remember if they had talked about his working today or not.

"Nope. I cleared the entire day." Gavin poured her a glass of orange juice.

The juice, followed by a cup of coffee, revived Madeline and brought back a recall of the previous night. She smiled, joining Gavin at the table to enjoy the omelettes and toast

She was on her way to her morning shower when Gavin called her back.

"Madeline, we forgot something," he said.

Madeline returned to the kitchen where Gavin stood by the table, a strip of bacon between his teeth.

"And what am I supposed to do about that, Mr. Marshall?" Madeline walked over to Gavin and put her arms around his waist, taking a minute to look into his eyes. "Wait a minute. I know." Then she closed her mouth around the other end of the bacon strip.

When their lips met, a lingering kiss ensued. Gavin and Madeline pulled away from the kiss, but their arms remained wrapped around each other.

"You fix a mean breakfast, Mr. Marshall," Madeline said. "Let's shower and then go for a ride."

"I've got a better idea," Gavin said, taking Madeline by the hand and leading her to the shower.

Chapter Eighteen

Madeline had no idea how soon her world would crash after her day of shared passion with Gavin.

Her mother and Emma Perry came home Tuesday afternoon, neither one richer, but both of them delighted after their adventure. They were already planning a future trip.

Work was going well, she was a new homeowner, and she and Gavin had a good chance now to work on building a relationship. *Yes,* Madeline thought on her way to work Wednesday, *life in Heron's Cove is good.*

****

On Wednesday after work, Gavin sat in Dennis's living room while Cody was playing at a neighbor's.

"Just how well do you know Madeline?" Dennis asked, looking at the envelope on his coffee table.

"She's got some problems, you know that, but she's working through them."

Dennis shook his head impatiently. "What I mean is, do you trust her?"

"Yeah," Gavin said. "I do."

"Well, this might change your mind." Dennis picked up the envelope and handed it to Gavin.

Gavin read the enclosed letter from Child Protective Services in Seattle before saying anything else. In a nutshell, it stated a complaint had been lodged against Dennis Garrett for the inability to parent his son, Cody Garrett. The letter had also stated, in part, that a caseworker would visit Heron's Cove on Monday with the goal of talking to those involved in Cody's life. Gavin wondered what Madeline would say about the caseworker. On the other hand, if she had filed the complaint, she already knew about the caseworker's pending visit. He was ashamed of the little fingers of doubt that were already poking at him, and he shook his head in an attempt to clear it of these thoughts.

"You can't possibly think it was Madeline," Gavin said.

"Man, you saw how she freaked at Cody's party. Who else would do this?"

"She didn't freak," Gavin said, "but I'll talk to her. As for who else would do this, I don't know. Madeline wouldn't have done this without talking to us first. She may be a lot of things, Denny, but underhanded isn't one of them."

"It figures you'd stick up for her," Dennis said. "You've been in her bed and your judgment is clouded."

Gavin stood up, seconds from punching his friend out. "Take that back, man," he said, his fists clenched in tight balls at his sides.

"I won't take it back. Go ahead. Punch me if you want. But it's true and you know it."

A war raged in Gavin as he rode home from his visit with Dennis. Things had been getting better for Madeline, and the possibility of them having a relationship, well...

No, damn it, I don't know it's true and neither does Denny. Would Madeline have filed a complaint like that without talking to either of them? She was pretty upset when we got drunk and didn't pick Cody up on time, but Madeline is direct. She would've told us she was going to file a complaint.

****

Madeline and her mother had dinner with Emma Perry on Wednesday, so Madeline wasn't home when Gavin called her. She hadn't bothered to take her cell phone, either. That said, Madeline was still blissfully unaware of the trouble headed her way.

It was eight o'clock when Madeline and her mother walked the short distance back to Madeline's house.

Sylvia pulled out her knitting, but not before checking the answering machine.

"You've got some messages, Madeline. Do you want me to listen?"

"Go ahead. They might be yours, Mom."

Madeline left the kitchen just in time to hear Gavin's

terse words punching her from the machine. "Madeline, call me."

"He certainly doesn't sound very happy," Madeline said. She wasn't really concerned, though, and made no move to pick up the phone.

"Aren't' you going to call Gavin back? He sounded upset."

"All right, Mom, I'll return his call." Madeline's hand was poised over the phone when it rang. Startled, she nearly dropped the phone in her effort to answer it.

"Hello?"

"Madeline, we have to talk," Gavin said.

"Okay. Tonight?"

"Yes tonight."

"Uh, do you want to come over here?" Madeline asked.

"Don't go anywhere," Gavin said. "I'll be there."

"That didn't sound like Gavin at all," Madeline said when she hung up. "He wasn't yelling or anything, but he sounded angry. I wonder what's up."

"I thought things were smoothing out between you," Sylvia said.

"I thought so, too, until tonight."

Gavin showed up less than fifteen minutes later, and though she didn't know what difference it made, Madeline was relieved to see that he had driven his truck.

Sylvia went to her room, allowing Gavin and Madeline some measure of privacy.

Without a word, Gavin handed an envelope to Madeline.

"Why are you giving me a letter addressed to Dennis?" she asked.

"Read it."

She pulled out the single page letter. When she finished reading, she looked at Gavin, a frown creasing her forehead.

"This is terrible, but I don't understand what it has to do with me."

"Dennis thinks you might've filed the complaint. Madeline, please tell me you had nothing to do with this."

Madeline saw a shadow that might have been pain

cloud Gavin's eyes, but she didn't care.

"It seems like you and Dennis have already decided I did this. Why should I say anything? That you even wonder if I did file is preposterous. What possible reason could I have for filing a complaint against Dennis?"

Gavin looked at her, the shadow lifted from his eyes. "Consider what happened Friday night," he reminded her. "And your brother's death alone is reason enough for you to have complained."

"I didn't file anything, but it's apparent I won't be able to convince you of that. However, here's something for you to think about. I've known for a while that you and Dennis pack Cody around on your bikes. Why would I wait until now to complain? And why would I have agreed to watch Cody on Friday?"

Gavin reached for Madeline's hand then, but she pulled away.

"Until this is straightened out, if then, I think it will be better if we don't see each other," she said.

Gavin left without a word.

Gavin's truck roared to life just before he sped down the street. Sylvia came out a few minutes later.

"I'm taking a wild guess here, but I don't think your meeting went well."

Madeline paced back and forth in the kitchen. "Good guess, Mom," she said, and proceeded to fill her mother in on the details of Gavin's brief visit.

"What are you going to do about it, Madeline?"

"Right now, Mom, I really don't know, but I do know this. After all this time I'm ready to leave the memory of Scott's accident in the past where it belongs and go forward with my life. It would be good if that life included Gavin, but I won't sit around waiting for it to happen."

****

Gavin didn't want to believe Madeline was in any way connected with the letter he had jammed back in his hip pocket on his way out of her house. Right now, however, no other explanation presented itself.

In addition, there was the whole other issue of how he felt about Madeline. He couldn't deny it any longer—he was falling in love with her. It looked like Dennis had been right about the dead-end road.

It was getting late, but instead of going home Gavin drove back to Dennis's house. Cody was already in bed when he got there.

"Denny, I just left Madeline's," Gavin said. "I don't think she filed the complaint." He told Dennis what Madeline had given him to think about.

"You may be right," Dennis said. "But who in hell would do it?"

"I don't know, buddy, but I think we have more thinking to do."

The next chance for the two men to talk came on Friday night after work as they combed through their respective memories, searching for any answer, any clue. Arrangements had been made earlier for Cody to spend the night with his best pal from daycare. Dennis and Gavin took Cody to his friend's house after dinner. On their way home, Dennis shared the conversation he'd had with Cody about the letter.

"Cody, I got a letter today, and I need to talk to you about it."

"Okay," Cody had said.

"Someone, I don't know who, made a report saying I'm not a good dad. That's what is in this letter."

"It's a lie. You're the best dad in the world."

Dennis was taken aback by the vehemence in his son's voice.

"The letter says a lady is coming on Monday to ask you and I some questions."

"What about?" Cody had asked. "Is she staying at our house?"

"About a report she got, and no, she won't stay here."

"Do I have to talk to her?"

"Yes, you do, Cody."

"What if I say something wrong?" Cody, eyes wide, had looked at his dad, perhaps searching for reassurance.

"Cody, just remember this. Whatever you tell that lady, be honest. Do you know what that means?"

Cody had nodded. "It means tell the truth."

When Dennis and Gavin got back to Dennis's house, Gavin noticed his friend's distraction.

"Hey, Denny, are you with me?"

"I'm here. I was just thinking about when I tried to explain the letter to Cody."

"Denny, what about Paula?"

"What about her?" Dennis asked.

"You said she was making noises about custody. She might've made the complaint," Gavin said.

Dennis looked at Gavin, a frown knitting his brows together.

"Yeah," Gavin said. "But think about this. That letter said pictures had been furnished that raised concerns about your ability to raise Cody and keep him safe."

"So?" Dennis was still frowning.

"Don't forget. Cody said that woman took his picture with Mako on his shoulder. Damn it! She put the camera away, but I took it away and had the film developed. Remember? There were only a couple of pictures of Cody holding Mako."

Dennis nodded. "But the letter says there are pictures. Where did they come from?" Dennis asked.

"I don't know," Gavin said. "Wait a minute. I might know after all. Remember at Murphy's when Cody told us that lady was in the parking lot?"

Dennis nodded.

"Well, Cody said it was the same lady who took his picture with Mako. I'll bet anything she was taking pictures as all of us arrived at Murphy's."

Gavin and Dennis fell silent, each man doing battle with his own thoughts.

"It definitely wasn't Paula who took that picture," Dennis said. "But it looks like she hired a private dick, or else got one of her druggie friends to do it."

"That woman who followed us everywhere on Friday night? At first I thought she was a local. We were well on our way to being drunk. Especially you."

"She wasn't hitting on us?" Dennis asked.

"Nope. Sorry buddy. Anyway, I remembered where I'd seen her before."

"Where?"

"She's the one who was taking Cody's picture," Gavin said, watching his friend anxiously as this new information dawned on him.

"And you didn't think it was important enough to tell me?"

"Face it, Denny. By the time I figured this out, you barely even knew what your name was or where you were. You weren't in any condition to process new information."

"So what now?" Dennis asked.

"I wish I had an answer," Gavin said.

After talking long into the night, Dennis and Gavin figured something else out.

"I better call Madeline tomorrow and apologize," Dennis said.

"Me, too," Gavin agreed, but he doubted whether Madeline would take his call.

****

Madeline had been conducting her own search for answers, and on Saturday morning she called Gavin.

"He's probably at work," she told her mother, expecting the inevitable answering machine to pick up. Instead, she heard,

"Talk to me."

"Gavin, it's Madeline. Do you have to work today?"

"Not until two. Why?"

"I need to talk to you about that letter."

"I'm listening," Gavin said.

"If it's all the same with you, I'd like to discuss it in person."

"Okay by me. Where?"

"Let's make it someplace neutral. How about Bisby's in half an hour?"

"Sounds good," Gavin said and he hung up.

Bisby's was a breakfast only café in Heron's Cove and normally busy, especially on weekends. After a short wait, Gavin and Madeline were shown to a booth.

When they had placed their orders, they sat quietly until Gavin broke the silence.

"It's good to see you, Madeline."

She smiled at Gavin, but there was little warmth in the gesture. "I'm here because I want to talk about the letter," she said.

154

"Understood." Gavin swallowed, his disappointment evident on his face.

"I'm curious about the pictures mentioned in the letter. Who could have taken them?"

Gavin shook his head. "I don't know. But, Madeline?"

"Yes?"

"I'm sorry for thinking you had anything to do with the complaint."

Their breakfasts arrived just then and even though they had little appetite for the food on the plates, Gavin and Madeline went through the pretense of eating.

"Didn't you say Cody got in trouble for talking to a stranger?" Madeline asked. Now that Gavin apologized she was having a difficult time concentrating on Cody and the letter. Was there hope after all for a relationship with Gavin?

Gavin, who had just put a forkful of food in his mouth, could only nod.

"Was it Dennis's ex-wife?"

"No," Gavin said. "She's in rehab."

"But you told me she has been out for a year."

"That's true," Gavin said. "But it wasn't Paula. You have to be sneaky to take pictures without being noticed. Trust me on this one. Paula isn't smart enough to be sneaky."

More eating followed until Gavin remembered something else, nearly shouting in his hurry to get the words out.

"Remember what Cody told me when we first got to his party?" Gavin asked.

Madeline thought for a split second. "You mean about that lady?"

"Right. He said it was the same person he talked to in front of his house. When I got outside, the parking lot was empty except for two or three vans."

"And right after you went out, Cody told me about his motorcycle," Madeline said. "He didn't say anything else about that woman. I should have asked him about her," Madeline finished lamely. "I'm sorry."

"It's okay, Madeline. Maybe we're getting to the bottom of this whole complaint thing."

Madeline insisted on paying for her own meal.

"Will you talk to the caseworker?" Gavin asked as he waited for Madeline to open her car door.

"I don't want to get involved," Madeline said.

"You already are," Gavin reminded her.

Madeline knew Gavin was right in spite of the fact she didn't know Cody or Dennis well at all. When this matter was wrapped, Madeline suspected she would have no further connection with the Garretts, or with Gavin Marshall.

****

Gavin went to Dennis's house Sunday. He hoped more talk would uncover some answers.

"You did what?" Gavin choked on a mouthful of coffee.

"You heard me," Dennis said. "When you told me everything Madeline said about all this, and what you figured out yesterday, I called Paula last night."

"She actually admitted to sending her friend down here?"

"Almost bragged about it, too. It was noisy in the background; there was a party going on, no doubt about it. Paula's using again. I'd bet on that."

Dennis and Gavin sat in silence, obviously each one thinking about what Dennis had just said.

"Hey, Gavin." Dennis broke the quiet.

"Yeah?"

"What are you still doing here? You need to square things with your lady."

Gavin's face was blank when he looked at Dennis.

"Madeline? She made it pretty clear she didn't want to talk to me unless it was about this case," Gavin said. "Seems like she should be the one to contact me."

"No way in hell should she contact you. Don't be a jackass, Gavin. It took a lot for Madeline to face the three of us and apologize for leaving the party. It's time you stepped up and called her. One thing's for sure. You won't work anything out with her if you just sit here."

Chapter Nineteen

"This is ridiculous," Madeline said as she and her mother were finishing breakfast Sunday morning.

"What's ridiculous?"

"Me acting like a child about talking to Gavin. Being afraid of things. All of it."

"So what are you going to do about it?" Madeline's mother asked.

"I'm going to call Gavin. For starters, I'll tell him I will talk to the caseworker and that I'm ready to talk to him." Madeline picked up the phone and punched in Gavin's cell number.

"Gavin, it's me. Just wanted you to know I'll talk to the caseworker. And, I...I want to see you again. Bye." Madeline said after she hung up, "Damn voicemail."

****

Gavin had a full slate of jobs on Sunday after he left Dennis's. He'd made up his mind to call Madeline, but when he flipped open his cell phone during a break he found he had a voicemail message waiting for him. His heart threatened to break out of his chest when he heard Madeline say she wanted to see him again. Gavin hit the speed dial number for Madeline's home phone.

"Hello?"

"Hi, Mrs. Spencer, it's Gavin. Is Madeline home?"

"Just a minute, Gavin. She's outside working in the flower beds."

It took Madeline only a few seconds to come inside and pick up the phone.

"Hello, Gavin. I'm glad you called back."

"This is the first break I've had today," Gavin said. "I was ready to call you when I saw I had voicemail."

"I just wanted to let you know I will talk to that caseworker tomorrow. I suppose it's too much to hope she won't ask me questions that will force me to talk about Scott's accident."

In spite of himself, Gavin couldn't help thinking, *not Scott again*. "I know it would hurt too much."

"No, it's not that. I don't want to say something that might hurt Dennis and Cody. Oh, I'm just being ridiculous. Of course I'll have to talk about the accident."

"Madeline no matter what the caseworker might ask you, just tell the truth."

"Gavin, let's get together. I really want to talk. About us."

"Okay. I'm working until eight tonight if you can believe that."

"Hmm. Now I feel a little guilty for doing as little as possible today," Madeline said. "Maybe tomorrow after work would be better. Are you working late tomorrow?"

"I have one job at five-thirty, but I'll reschedule it," Gavin said.

"Don't do that, Gavin. Your work is important. Would you like to come over here for dinner after you finish the job?"

"How about if you come to my place and I'll cook dinner for you? It probably wouldn't be until seven, seven-thirty, though."

"Fine with me," Madeline said.

"Oh. What about your mother?" Gavin asked.

"What about her?"

"Well...uh...I mean..."

Madeline laughed then, but softly. "Gavin, it's okay if we have dinner without my mother. I'm pretty sure she would insist we have dinner without her."

"Well, okay then," Gavin said. "I'll pick you up as soon as I'm through work."

****

After the phone call, Madeline found her mother reclining on a chaise lounge on the back deck. Madeline snagged two diet sodas from the fridge and joined her.

"You look happier than I've seen you in a while," Madeline's mother said.

"I feel better than I have in quite some time. Gavin is picking me up when he's through work tomorrow and he's cooking dinner for me." Madeline settled herself in her seat with a smile on her face. "More importantly, we're going to talk about us. Mom, I'm ready to admit I love Gavin and I am going to tell him."

"Good for you, Madeline. May I add, it's about time."

"I don't know how Gavin will react when I tell him, but I know this is something I need to do. I'm prepared to deal with whatever the results are.

"You know, Mom, maybe I won't have to talk to that caseworker." Even as she said the words Madeline knew how untrue they sounded.

"Don't count on it," her mother said.

Madeline laughed. "I'm not. As I said I knew it was wishful thinking. Cody told that woman I cut the bird's wings, so a note has undoubtedly been made about animal cruelty."

"Don't blame Cody," her mother said.

"Of course I don't blame him. He shouldn't have talked to a stranger the way he did, but he's just a little boy. He said what he did in childish innocence."

When Madeline went to work Monday morning, her one hope was that the caseworker wouldn't be in Heron's Cove until late morning, or maybe early afternoon. That hope was dashed when Kelly told her at nine o'clock that she had a call on line one.

"And it isn't Gavin," Kelly said.

Madeline picked up the phone expecting a question or comment about a pet.

"This is Dr. Spencer. May I help you?"

"Hello, Dr. Spencer. This is Carolyn Shays from Child Protective Services in Seattle. I imagine you know why I'm calling."

"Yes, I do," Madeline said.

"Would there be a convenient time for us to meet today?"

"I have some free time at one," Madeline told her.

"Fine. I'll see you at one."

Madeline shook her head. "I figured she wouldn't be in town until later today, but she must have come in last night."

Kelly was standing by and when she spoke, she

offered encouragement. "You'll be fine, Madeline. I'm rooting for you and so is Joe."

At precisely one o'clock, a woman about Madeline's age walked through the doors of Heron's Cove Veterinary Hospital.

Madeline didn't need to see the woman's briefcase or her businesslike demeanor to know Carolyn Shays had arrived.

"May I help you?" Madeline asked.

"I'm here to see Dr. Spencer," the woman said.

"I'm Dr. Spencer," Madeline said, extending her hand.

"Carolyn Shays. Is there somewhere private where we can talk?"

Madeline led the way to her office and closed the door.

"Would you like something to drink?" Madeline asked before she sat down behind her desk.

"Thank you. No." Carolyn Shays sat in one of the visitor's chairs across from Madeline's desk.

"I'd like to ask you some questions about Cody Garrett and his father, Dennis Garrett."

Whoa, she cuts right to the chase.

"Fine," Madeline said.

"Dennis Garrett is a single father and he works full time. Who watches Cody?"

"Cody is in a fine daycare center while his father works," Madeline said.

"Do you think Dennis Garrett is putting his son in danger?"

"No," Madeline said.

"He carries his son around on his motorcycle. You don't consider that a danger, Dr. Spencer?"

Madeline counted to ten before she answered. Questions were one thing. This woman's apparent attack on motorcycles was uncalled for.

"No, Ms. Shays, I don't. By the laws of this state, Cody is old enough to ride as a passenger. When he does, his father sees to it that Cody wears a helmet, leather jacket, chaps, boots and gloves."

"Do you ride, Dr. Spencer?"

"Yes, I do."

"So your opinion in this matter is necessarily biased."

"I don't think that's necessarily true," Madeline said, putting extra weight on necessarily. "I think I'm capable of making unbiased judgments."

Careful, Madeline. This woman is getting to you. Don't let that happen. At least don't let her see she is.

"You're aware of the statistics on motorcycle accidents and fatalities?"

"I'm well aware of the statistics, Ms. Shays."

"Do you have a lot of riding experience?" Ms. Shays' condescending tone set Madeline's teeth on edge.

"Let's see," Madeline began. "I started riding when I was five years old, under strict supervision by my parents. I'm thirty-one now." Madeline was starting to enjoy this interview. "So yes, I have a few years' experience."

"Have you ever been in a motorcycle accident?" The caseworker's tone changed little.

"No."

"Do you know anyone who has been involved in a motorcycle accident?"

She really doesn't waste much time, does she? "Yes," Madeline said. "My brother was killed when he was seventeen and I was twenty. A drunk driver rear-ended his bike. I was riding with him and saw the whole thing."

"I'm sorry," Ms Shays offered. "In spite of this, you still don't have a problem with Cody Garrett riding a motorcycle with his father?"

"To say I'm not concerned at all would be ludicrous. There's a risk factor in most activities we undertake, including motorcycle riding. We just need to practice reasonable precaution and common sense."

"If Cody Garrett was your son, would you feel the same way?"

"Yes, Ms. Shays, I would."

"Well, it looks like I'm finished here." Carolyn Shays stood, offering her hand to Madeline. "It was good meeting you, Dr. Spencer."

Madeline shook the other woman's hand. "I'll walk you out," she said.

The remainder of the day kept Madeline busy

tending animal patients and for that she was grateful. She was, however, more than ready to go home at five.

While she waited for Gavin to pick her up, Madeline filled her mother in on the events of the day.

"I don't believe it, Mom. For the entire hour she was in my office she asked more questions about motorcycles than anything else."

When Gavin came by, the three of them chatted for a few minutes before Gavin and Madeline left.

"Did Carolyn Shays talk to you today?" Madeline asked on the way to Gavin's house.

"Who?"

"That caseworker," Madeline said.

"Nah. I get the privilege tomorrow morning at ten. Was it really awful, Madeline?"

"No, I can't say it was awful. More weird and unsettling than anything else."

"How so?" Gavin asked.

"She asked more motorcycle questions than anything. I felt like I was being investigated."

"Did she ask about Scott's accident?"

"Not directly, but the subject did come up." Madeline told Gavin about the rest of her time with Carolyn Shays.

"I'm worried about what will happen to Cody if things go badly and he is sent to live with his mother. Of course, I'm also worried about what that would do to Denny."

"Gavin, you and I together will do what we can to keep Dennis and Cody from being separated."

When they got to his house, Gavin stopped the truck in the driveway and went around to open Madeline's door.

The minute she stepped inside, Madeline felt the masculine strength in Gavin's house. Just like Gavin she thought.

"Why did you decide to talk to the caseworker after you said you didn't want to get involved?" Gavin asked as he and Madeline walked to the living room after dinner.

They sat on the leather sofa, each aware of the physical distance between them, but knowing the time wasn't right to close it.

"I realize how important your friendship with Dennis is and I know he and Cody will always be a part of your life. I thought what I knew about motorcycles might help them."

"You did everything you could." Gavin's voice was soft.

Madeline looked at him, her expression tinged with amazement. "How can you know that? You weren't in the room with us."

"Because you've stepped over some big hurdles in the last few weeks," Gavin said.

Madeline shifted her position on the couch so that she faced Gavin.

"So many people stood by me and tried to help after Scott's accident, and I wouldn't let them. All I did was push them away. Still, they didn't give up." Madeline sighed deeply. "Maybe I just got comfortable wrapped up in the 'poor me' routine. But no more. My brother's memory will always be a part of my life, but I refuse to let that memory control my life any more and push aside the people I love."

Madeline straightened her shoulders and looked in Gavin's incredible eyes. "One of those people is you, Gavin. I knew almost from the first time we met that I was falling in love with you. The fall is complete now."

Gavin sat quietly. *Please say something, Gavin, anything...*

"When I came home from the war, I didn't want to get involved with anyone, male or female. But for starters, Denny was already a solid part of my life and when Cody was born, he was like a part of me, too. Then I met you, Madeline. There wasn't a time when I didn't want to be with you. Even when I thought you might have turned Dennis in."

"I love you, Gavin. I can't promise anything, but I want us to have a chance to work things out."

"I understand. I want that same chance for us to be together. Madeline, I love you."

Gavin held out his arms and Madeline went into them without hesitation. There was no music playing in the background, but Gavin and Madeline didn't need it.

Epilogue

Although Gavin and Madeline were kept busy with
their respective jobs, they rode every day the weather
permitted, including a trip to Florida to visit Gavin's
father. Madeline also agreed to share her racing
knowledge with Cody.

One night, just before Thanksgiving, Gavin planned
a surprise dinner for Madeline. During dinner, the
conversation turned to all of the big events during the last
couple of months.

Joe and Kelly had gotten married, and Kelly applied
to veterinary school at Washington State University.

Sylvia Spencer moved to Heron's Cove and bought
Madeline's house. She had also agreed to fill in as a
receptionist at the veterinary hospital once Kelly started
school and a permanent replacement could be found.

Carolyn Shays took a week to complete her
interviews, and it was another week before a decision was
handed down. She concluded there was no basis for the
original complaint against Dennis and the matter was
dropped.

After the meal, Madeline curled up next to Gavin,
her head resting on his shoulder.

"Gavin, this has been a pretty exciting time but the
best part has been the time spent with you."

"I have to be the happiest man who ever drew
breath," Gavin said, his arm around Madeline.

"Why do you say that?"

"Because you stood by me, because you love me."

"It hasn't always been easy." She chuckled and
burrowed in closer.

"If I'm dreaming and I wake up by myself, then I
hope it's a dream I have every night," Gavin said.

"You aren't dreaming," Madeline said. "I'm really

here, and when you wake up in the morning, I'll still be here."

"I love you, Madeline. When you're not with me, I feel empty. As much as I love riding, without you it doesn't mean as much, and I never thought I'd say those words." Gavin reached behind the couch and picked something from the windowsill. He handed a small box to Madeline.

"What's this?"

"It's a little something for your birthday."

"But you sent me the beautiful roses and prepared dinner."

"I know, but I wanted to give you something to unwrap."

Madeline's fingers trembled slightly as she slid the ribbon from the package and undid the paper. She lifted the lid to reveal a small, maroon velvet box. Inside that was a diamond ring.

"I want you in my life, for the rest of my life, Madeline. Will you marry me?"

Tears flowing down her cheeks, Madeline held out her left hand so Gavin could put the ring on her finger. No words could express all of the emotions she felt but her heart knew this devil in her arms.

A word about the author...

Patty drew on her love for motorcycles to write her first romance novel. She and her husband, Eldon, live in Long Beach, Washington. They have two grandchildren.

Printed in the United States
95275LV00001B/34-81/A